Angola
Is Wherever I
Plant My Field

Angola Is Wherever I Plant My Field

Stories

JOÃO MELO

TRANSLATED BY LUÍSA VENTURINI

ISKANCHI
PRESS AND MAG

Published in 2022 by Iskanchi Press
info@iskanchi.com
https://iskanchi.com/

ISBN: 978-1-957810-01-0

Printed in the United States of America

Contents

The Revolutionary Duck and the Counter-Revolutionary Duck

To Kassessa

*A*ngolans—in addition to loving makas,[1] partying till morning, arriving late for appointments, and using and abusing humor even against themselves—were post-modern before the concept was even invented. Iconoclasts, they don't take anything too seriously to the point of behaving like jerks—this term may not be very literary, but what to do when the writer himself is Angolan?—when it comes to the lessons, the rules, and the models that the world has been trying to impose on them forever.

Contemporary history is full of examples that confirm the profound and multiple irresponsibility of Angolans.

---

1   Maka is a Kimbundu word for a rather delicate and serious problem.

Firstly, when millions were taken to the Americas as slaves, not only did they resist being completely destroyed by brutal exploitation and unknown diseases such as influenza and syphilis, but they taught their very oppressors how to forge iron, extract diamonds and gold from the ground and how to plant (and harvest) sugar cane and coffee.

They also taught the oppressors how to play and dance to the ancestral rhythms they carried in their blood and which they spread from the cotton fields in the North of the American continent to the pampas in the South. They reinvented the languages imposed upon them, introducing thousands of new words and expressions. They contributed to the Africanization of the Indo-European religions they encountered across the new continent. They created heroes like Zumbi, in Brazil, and the nineteen Angolans who contributed to the fight for independence in Chile. Finally, they transformed the vast and sunny region between the Caribbean and Brazil into a warehouse full of mixed-race girls, quite correctly considered to be an authentic global product nowadays.

Meanwhile, those who stayed in their homeland welcomed the foreign aggressors in a way that will remain forever in the annals of human conviviality: fighting them fiercely, they nevertheless did business with them; handing over their daughters for marriage; adopting their religions while teaching them ghostly rituals that would drive them crazy; tasting the aggressors' wishy-washy wine while offering them their own unknown drinks to taste; and lastly, taking them into the depths of the most remote parts of their country, where they would get yellow fever and die hopelessly. For those who are unaware, I should add that these different and multiple strategies were not used alternately but simultaneously, to the despair of the invaders who, to this day, have been utterly unable to get to fully know the Angolans, particularly their instinct for survival and their flexibility.

One particularly incomprehensible detail for the aforementioned invaders was how, in the course of this extraordinary process, the Angolans were mixing not only among themselves but with the invaders too, both killing and desperately fornicating with them, thus swallowing each other up in an incredible history of blood and laughter, crime and redemption, all the time making them more and more Angolan. As proof that extreme ends really do meet, this is considered the height of irresponsibility, not only by past invaders but also by contemporary ultra-nationalist and neo-racist cazumbis.[2]

More recently, Angolans were the authors of two of the most prodigious operations of social engineering in contemporary history: they transformed Marxist-Leninist socialism into a schematic socialism, and neo-liberal capitalism into mafia capitalism. Some authors call the former Afro-Stalinism and the latter savage capitalism, but these are ideological titles without any use whatsoever, and fine post-modern literature should not waste time on them.

---

2   Cazumbis refers to ghosts.

If comrade Chung Park Lee knew a little bit of Angolan history—not the one taught in the guides and manuals, but the everyday one which, in truth, is yet to be written because that task would require overcoming several general prejudices and preconceptions—he would have been immediately wary of the question asked by the MPLA guerrilla, who arrived in North Korea only two weeks earlier for his military training:

—*If a drake lays an egg on the border between North and South Korea, who owns the* egg?

Comrade Lee felt, as we say, like scratching his head. He had just sat himself down, having just given a class about the historic treason of the South Korean regime, whose leaders were no more than a bunch of hawkers who had submitted themselves to the abominable and detestable imperialism of North America. During that class, he had told the students—a bunch of young revolutionaries who came from various areas of the then so-called Third World, from neighboring Vietnam to far-away Nicaragua, and all of whom were understandably well-intentioned like all young people, whether revolutionaries or not—to feel free to ask any questions and express any doubts.

—*Come again?* he asked, while considering the best answer to such an unusual question.

—*It's very simple!* said the young Angolan guerrilla. *Just imagine, Comrade Professor, that a drake lays an egg very precisely on the border between North and South Korea. To which country does the egg belong?*

The teacher could not resist it and scratched himself

discreetly before replying with as much certainty as he could:

—*Well, surely the egg would be a little bit more on this side, so it could only belong to North Korea.*

—*No, no… The egg was laid exactly in the middle of the border, not even a millimeter nearer their side or our side…*

—*In that case*, said the professor, *the drake must have been fleeing from South Korea to join the glorious revolution of the Korean people led by our Great Leader, Comrade President Kim Il Sung. Therefore, the egg must have belonged to North Korea.*

The inquisitive guerrilla must have been from Malanje or Catete because, according to the idiosyncratic map of Angolan people, the inhabitants of both towns always think they are smarter than everyone else. Speaking almost in a whisper and choosing his words carefully, with a slightly mocking if discreet look in his eyes, he insisted:

—*Comrade Professor, I'm so sorry, but the drake was not leaving South Korea since he was from North Korea… This was a revolutionary duck!*

The professor responded instinctively, if not mechanically:

—*He was a traitor! If he laid an egg on the border that means that he was attempting to flee…*

—*I don't disagree, Comrade Professor! But you have still not answered the question. What about the egg?*

Comrade Chung Park Lee thought, with some surprise, that the young MPLA guerrilla wanted to test his loyalty to the just cause of the Korean Revolution and to the teachings of the Great Leader, Kim Il Sung. Therefore, he decided to end this sorry joke once and for all. Almost shrieking, he said:

—*The drake was a counter-revolutionary! But, no matter what, our brave fighters guarding the border would never have allowed the southern henchmen to take hold of that egg!*

On hearing such a definite and forceful statement, it was now the Angolan guerrilla who was shocked. He could imagine the egg full of holes in the middle of the border, in the security zone between the two Koreas, while the poor duck was destroyed, its feathers everywhere, making small and clumsy movements followed by howls and painful screams coming from its throat. A sticky white and yellow halo spread across the ground, further and further, and changing color as it grew in circles. Rapidly, the egg-white and the yolk, now completely broken up, had become all mixed up with the blood of the duck, forever sacrificed by the prompt revolutionary alertness of the Korean guards. "*So, in the end, is that what Revolution means?*" he asked himself before responding to Comrade Lee.

Without wishing to delay his response too much more, the narrator is nevertheless obliged to make a short interruption at this point in the story to give—in two or three short lines—a brief profile of the young guerrilla because this may be useful for understanding his, let's say, existential doubt about the fate of the egg. Pedro Muanza Agostinho—this is what he was called—was an eighteen-year-old former student who aligned himself with the MPLA so as to help realize a dream that, in those times, was devoutly shared by most Angolans: to expel the Portuguese colonizers and turn Angola into an independent country. As a result, he only had a vague idea about why and for what he joined, and he only knew the sound of the words with which he had started to become acquainted when he joined the movement, such as "socialism" and "Revolution". A few months after arriving in Congo, where the guerrilla bases were, he was sent to North Korea—a revolutionary, anti-imperialistic country, he was told—to complete a six-month military training course.

Pedro arrived in North Korea full of questions. However, the absurd discussion with comrade Chung Park Lee made him wonder if his questions would ever be answered. Since he was only eighteen, he could not fully understand the long-term implications of this. Because of this, he decided to checkmate comrade Lee. Being the good Angolan he was, he made his move with all the serenity in the world, enjoying each word as if it were a physical orgasm:

—*I am sorry to inform you, Comrade Professor, but drakes do not lay eggs. Only hens do!*

What happened next can be told in three paragraphs.

Comrade Chung Park Lee, mortified by the Angolan, prepared a report for the department of Foreign Affairs of the Party, thereby submitting the subject for discussion at the meeting of the Secretariat, which, having analyzed it, forwarded it to the next session of the Central Committee to be held two weeks later, accompanied by a full dossier in which, among many diverse, precious and absolutely rigorous and objective pieces of information, comrade Pedro Muanza Agostinho—the Angolan guerrilla sent by MPLA to complete a six-month military training in the Democratic People's Republic of Korea—was charged with attempting to facilitate the escape of a North Korean duck to the territory illegally controlled by the henchmen of North American imperialism. In addition to that—and confirmed in the dossier—this same comrade had the habit of asking his teachers very provocative questions, and they didn't know what to do because his questions had not been discussed in any of the teaching guides prepared by the Great Leader, Kim Il Sung.

To these gravest of charges were added the otherwise unknown fact that, just two weeks after his arrival, comrade Agostinho had organized a party in his dormitory, to which he had invited trainees from Cuba, Brazil, Mexico, Congo, Cape Verde, and other irresponsible Third World countries. At these parties, weird rhythms were played and the young trainees danced lustfully, ate and drank like the bourgeoisie, and fornicated with the most outrageous pleasure and joy. When the orgies were over—commented the shocked author of the dossier—comrade Agostinho could be heard laughing extremely loudly as he passed through the hallways of the academy.

The verdict was harsh. The young Angolan guerrilla was found innocent of the charge of attempting to facilitate the duck's escape "*due to the absence of proof of evidence.*" He was, however, found guilty of all the other charges, meaning all those mentioned in the dossier and a few others which, with improvised creativity, had been specially formulated for his case: specifically, that he had not mastered the basics of revolutionary zoology and had ignored the fact that in the Korean workers' homeland drakes can lay eggs thanks to theories developed by the Great Leader, Comrade Kim Il Sung. He would therefore have to be expelled and sent back to Angola. Thus, less than a month after his departure, Pedro Muanza Agostinho returned to his traditional MPLA base in Dolisie, Congo.

This story took place in the 1960s, the high point of the two main metanarratives that had been fighting each other for the past two hundred years. Back then, nobody knew what a metanarrative was because, in the name of the two great ideologies of the day—liberalism and Marxism—men confronted each other physically, on the battlefield, and the deadly weapons they used to eliminate each other were obviously not simply for linguistic games. Meanwhile, an unknown Angolan guerrilla, who only today makes his entrance into world literature, anticipated Lyotard, managing to demonstrate through an apparently naive riddle, how grandiloquent speeches can be distorted and perverted in practice to become imitations of reality.

Isn't that amazing?

As far as I'm concerned, I firmly believe that this story will be included as part of a collection of exemplary post-modern short stories. But if it does not satisfy you, readers, you at least need to know what happened to the young MPLA guerrilla and to the Korean professor whom he so valiantly confronted during the pure and difficult times of that epoch, by calling a spade a spade and ruthlessly deconstructing the rigidity of the professor's monolithic revolutionary speech.

During the early 1990s, comrade Chung Park Lee defected to South Korea where he became a senior executive in a large agriculture and poultry farming company. By the end of the decade, his company signed a contract with the Angolan government and, having sent the former professor of history of the Korean revolution to Angola as the local head of the company, set up an office there. Although he reached the rank of commander during the Angolan guerrilla war, Pedro Muanza Agostinho had not managed in the meantime to become one of the country's neo-capitalists. The courage he had shown during the struggle for independence, when he engaged resolutely in the fight against the colonizers, was no longer there. And I will tell you candidly that he was unable to take from the pocket of the state and turn himself into a private landlord, unlike some other former revolutionaries. Since he had joined the technical staff of the company that was now granted to the Koreans to develop, he ironically found himself an employee of Mister Lee. This is even more amazing than the supposedly post-modern nature of this story.

Ah! I almost forgot to mention this: the core business of this new company was raising ducks.

Sir, Give Me Just a Fiver

Translated by Lara Pawson

S ir, give me just a fiver, just a fiver, really, to buy some bread, I'm hungry, I still haven't eaten anything since the day before yesterday, the other kids caught me out at caçambula,[3] they got the cash that a chief had given me, I saw him when he arrived with his babe, she could have been his daughter, or grand-daughter, I dunno, he left his car down there close to the boulders, I waited a while, counting on my fingers, I know how to count, sir, I went to school too, I reached fourth grade, a b c d, one two three four, like that sir, just like that, yes sir, don't laugh, it was my teacher who said it, there in the bush where I was before I came here to Luanda as a displaced person, some said I was a displaced, others a refugee, we never heard these words in the bush, even in school we didn't see or hear them, but, well, there in the bush, folks didn't know

---

3   A children's game whose aim is to trick opponents into dropping an object or giving it away by mistake. The object could be food, a ball, money, a hat, anything.

these words and they also didn't get to eat, it's only here that we eat, alas, you're laughing sir, really laughing, you don't know that there is refugee food and displaced food and food of the tattered and the torn, of the down-and-out, we look for it every night in the garbage containers, we fight over it, crippling ourselves, but still finding good stuff, chicken bones like recyclable ribbons, yes sir, recyclable, I learned this word from some of the guys who hang out here, they turn up on mopeds saying, *We're from the Green Gang*, I think it's odd that in the middle of all these blacks and mixed races there's a couple of whiteys, they say, *We have here some seedlings for you to plant,* we look at them in a way they don't get, they're thickheads, among us we kiss our teeth, trees, trees, we want them but not to eat, although we are still hungry, starving with hunger, our hunger is so bad that we could kill these green guys, they're all so nutritious, so delicious, so fragrant, even so the best thing is to go back to rummaging through our containers, sometimes we even find a few good things like cow meat that's so old you don't even need to chew it, just swallow and hey presto, pieces of bread so riddled with holes they look like they've been shot at, cans of beer, cans of fizzy drinks, cans of sardines, cans of tuna, cans of beans, cans of fruit, cans of candy, so many cans, cans, I reckon the whole world is one big canning factory, the only problem is the rats, the dogs, the cats, even the crooks are pretty bold, we have to yell at them, the other day Filipe said, *These sons of bitches are creating unfair competition*, I laughed, mostly because I don't know what unfair

means, but I laughed because that day I'd also had nothing
to eat, I thought, fuck, one day I'm going to grab one of
those big rats that turn up and eat the cats and I'm going
to make a beast of a barbecue, eating only a little bit and
selling the rest in tiny pieces, if I'd done this today I
wouldn't need to ask you, sir, give me just a fiver, really
only a fiver, sir, the shame is in thieving not asking, I
haven't eaten anything since the day before yesterday, not
even bread drenched in liquid, bugs, bad smells, shit, no,
for fuck's sake, don't mess me, my friends stole the money
that the chief gave me, I counted on the fingers of my
hands, I worked out that the guy must have had his dick
out of his trousers by then, he must have asked the chick
to suck him off already, and she'd probably never even
seen a porn film before, but what am I supposed to make
of this, nothing, sir, nothing, I myself am already
completely fucked off with my life, like the other day, I
swear, I was a hungry son-of-a-bitch, I watched the chief
maneuvering his car with his lights off, then parking up
and turning off the engine, I hung back, counting up to
ten on my fingers, then approaching the car almost
without breathing or touching the ground, I didn't just go
to school, sir, I also know how to walk on water like Jesus,
the priest said that, I got to the car window and knocked
once, but the guy didn't open it, I knocked twice, same
thing, I thought this bastard doesn't know who I am, just
because he's a chief he thinks I'm dumb or what, I began
hitting the windows without stopping, then the doors and
the bonnet, the guy got out, all out of breath and into the

bargain, without noticing that his prick was still poking out, sir, ah ah ah, his stick was so tiny, like mine, ah ah ah, the poor girl, I thought, if you've got to start fucking at least do it with a quality love-stick, but before the chief could open his mouth I pointed my pistol at him, I spoke with such a low voice you could hardly hear me, *Sir give me just a fiver,* with my hand firm on the gun but my voice just a tiny trickle, eyes fixed, dulled like an insect's, I am an insect, sir, miserable vermin, but there with the gun in my hand I seemed more like a commandant, shouting down at the chief, his knob still hanging out of his trousers, completely shriveled, totally limp, unworthy of any comment, *Put that piece of crap away, for fuck's sake, put it away before I castrate you right here right now, shit man, so your wife knows that you're here does she, with your grand-daughter, cos this girl is young enough to be your grandchild, you dick, your wife knows, huh, she knows, huh, get back inside, go on, get inside,* I swear, sir, the chief looked like horse shit, he backed up real slow, *easy boy, easy, be careful with that weapon, let's talk, how much is it that you'd like exactly, a fiver, only a fiver, take it, you can count it, there's five hundred there, lower the gun, hey, lower the gun,* the guy thinks I'm from the bush or what, *get inside, go on, back up, get inside,* the fool fell back into the car seat, noticing his prick for the first time, he quickly zipped up his trousers, pushing his shirt in nice and tight, *Give me just a fiver,* I said, the barrel of the gun was pressing against his head by now, my voice was still weak but my pulse, sir, I swear, I don't know how to explain it but my pulse was getting stronger and stronger, not just a tremor, it seemed like it was from the gasoline I'd been sniffing all afternoon to forget my hunger, my pulse was strong enough to compensate my voice which was weak, *Give me just a fiver you son-of-a-bitch, give me just a fiver,* the bastard could tell from the trickle of my voice that I was faking it, he only pulled out his papers and I let it go, sir, I let it go because deep down I'm just a good kid, I don't want to hurt anyone, just because everyone hurts me, one day I'll find out, sir, I swear it, sir, I'm going to find out why the whole world has done me wrong, the guy threw the bag with all his money in front of the car, I didn't move an inch, *Turn the key you bastard,* I pushed the barrel of the gun a bit harder, *but don't start up without my say-so,* all of a sudden sir, I don't know how to explain this either, I hadn't been thinking anything, all I wanted was a fiver to buy some bread, but all of a sudden, and it really was all of a sudden I swear, I didn't want it, I looked at the babe all hunched up on the other seat, she must have been fifteen, not pretty, not ugly, but she was wearing a mini-skirt that was barely a skirt, it was just a mini, her thighs already shapely, I looked at her long and hard, she looked like a little animal lost in the forest, she could have been my sister, sir, since I've been in Luanda because of the war I don't know where my sisters are any more, but that chick could easily have been one of my sisters, all of a sudden I wanted to cry, I don't know if the guy noticed but I acted real quick, I pointed the gun in the direction of the girl and said, *You stay here, go, you get out of the car, don't be fucking afraid, this bastard isn't going to do anything to you, if he wants a*

*fuck he can fuck his own woman at home, go girl, get out of the car,
and you, my son-of-a-bitch, keep quiet, keep quiet or I'll blow
your brains out right this minute,* all of a sudden, sir, I myself
don't know how to explain this because everything
happened so fast, the chief cried out *Aninhas, don't leave,*
and ducked his head to avoid the barrel of the gun while
sticking his left leg out of the car kicking me in the knees,
I lost my balance a bit, ah, sir, that afternoon I'd sniffed a
lot of gasoline, my pulse was strong, without a tremor, sir,
without regret, sir, when I opened my eyes the chief's
head was on the steering wheel, blown to bits, blood was
spurting from his forehead on to the carpet forming a
little pool that was getting steadily larger, the chick was
completely crumpled up on the other side of the car,
hunched up in fear, paralyzed by her own screams, without
the strength to open the door and vanish, it would have
been better if she'd disappeared, sir, but she didn't, it
looked like she was waiting for her own misfortune or
perhaps someone sent her to ruin my life just a little bit
more, I went round the other side of the car, I opened her
door and said, *Let's get the hell out of here, girl,* before the riot
cops turn up, only that instead of obeying me she had a
really weird reaction, throwing herself against my chest,
she began to scratch me and kick me in the shins, *You killed
my friend, you killed my friend, he was going to sort me out, he
was going to give me a child,* while she was yelling tears were
running down her face, every now and then she tried to
get the gun out of my hand, *Calm,* I was saying, *calm down
girl, it was him who asked to be killed, who made me react, I only*

16

wanted a fiver to buy some bread, and then she said, *why did you kill him,* this question left me speechless, sir, how was I going to explain to her that it wasn't simply a question of dough, you know my life is well and truly more complicated than that, so I said to her, more calmly, *Who let him bring you here to fuck you like this in the middle of the street,* the chick looked at me as if I was from another world or perhaps some TV character, *Don't you have anything, she asked, anything at all,* I went all floppy, all my strength disappeared out of my legs, it went all dark inside my head, I grabbed her by the wrists and pinned her to my chest, the pistol fell on to the sand from the beach, I didn't look, I simply felt her tears in my hair, I embraced her with all my strength, my tears also began to fall very slowly from my eyes, all of a sudden I began to remember a pile of things, for example, one day I was in Chitepa with my two younger brothers, I looked at them and said someday I am going to Luanda to see the sea, they laughed knowing that our father was never going to let me go, but that day I got on the WFP plane like a refugee, or a displaced person, whichever, and I jolly well came to Luanda, no one had heard from my father, he had gone to work in his field three days earlier and he still hadn't returned home the day I got on the plane and began to howl for my parents who'd been killed by some bandits, just take me away, I don't have any parents any more, their names, ah, their names, my father is António Canivete João, my mother, Andua, but they're both dead I know it, just take me, I don't know if my father already knows that I now am also a Luandan, when I arrived I was a bit surprised but soon enough I got a hold of the situation, first they put me in a house full of priests but I fled on the third day, now I'm here on the Ilha, I have my own hole in the ground,[4] I go out during the day to my odd jobs, at night I stay here to look after the cars that turn up for all sorts of shenanigans, they don't take any notice when I sidle up to them ever so quietly, saying, sir give me just a fiver, some of them leap into action like wild goats, searching for their shirt or trousers, the chicks always shrink back, covering their eyes with their hands, suddenly going even quieter than if they were dumb, but I act as if I haven't seen anything, I repeat, sir, only a fiver, I gently extend my hand, sometimes I wait an eternity, but most cough up quickly just to get rid of me, with the most stubborn I pull out my gun and ask, *Are you deaf or what, give me a fiver or I'll put a hole in you right away,* I was remembering, sir, the chick pinned ever more tightly to my chest, I heard my mother's voice, the cries of my mother, all her despair when those men assaulted her, one, two, three, four, five, six, after sticking a bayonet inside her snatch they poured gasoline over her and set her on fire, my older brother and I were hiding in the long grass behind the house, we saw everything, we wanted to save our mother but we ran, we ran, we ran until we ran into soldiers, ever since then I have heard my mother's voice inside my head, rising all of a sudden at the worst

---

4   Some street children in Luanda live beneath the streets in drains and large potholes.

moments when I would rather die, as I did that night when I put a bullet into the chief with the Mercedes and now his chick is in my arms, all fragile and weak thinking that maybe I was really strong simply because I had a gun and had done away with her sugar daddy, what she didn't realize is that I am even more fragile than her, my head was far away remembering the day I decided to run away from Chitepa, it was an ordinary day, the same as all the others, nobody saw any strange signs in the air, my father received some visitors, they went to a corner of the main room, they drank cachipembe, they talked in low voices, nobody heard a thing, after, when the visitors had left, he said I'm going to the fields, three days passed, there was no sign of him, my mother had already died, my brothers were in a daze, motionless, doing nothing, I asked if they were waiting for father but they didn't respond, the look they gave was whitened, as if they were under a spell, my sisters were dragging themselves about on the floor, covered in snot and flies and tears, it was the hunger, sir, the world there in Chitepa was one simply of hunger and silence, the only ones who stayed were the elderly and the children, the women who managed to avoid being abused like my mother were seized in the light of day, the men would say they were going to their fields and would disappear, so I took a decision, I'm not waiting any longer, I took the WFP plane and, hey, after I arrived in Luanda, a few months later, a cousin of mine turned up, he's like a brother, he told me uncle António had joined UNITA, oh brother, I felt nothing, neither sadness nor happiness, nothing sir, but later when I was alone I asked myself but who is my father, he went to the fields long ago, I don't remember him anymore, I only remember my mother, they raped her, they shoved a bayonet up her cunt and afterwards, as a final insult, they burned her, for fuck's sake, sir, how could my father join UNITA, how, so I decided to forget everything, even my name, you can call me whatever you wish sir, but that night when I extinguished the chief with three bullets in his head, his bitch reminded me of my sisters, ah, sir, sometimes I have such unbelievable saudades,[5] but only for them, so that night I led the girl away as carefully as I could, with all the sweetness I had left in me but also with grief, I led her away from the dead body of that son-of-a-bitch, that randy rascal, that shameless old codger, and we went to the beach, I took off her clothes, I screwed her, I screwed her, I screwed her, it seemed as though I wasn't actually shagging her but was taking my revenge on the world, she didn't say a thing, she only cried and laughed and suddenly began to shout out, give me a child, give me a child, I shouted with her, *why father, why father*, when we had finished we rested a while in the sand, side by side relishing the moment, afterwards we got up in silence, we plunged into this sea of Luanda, we swam, we played, we washed ourselves well, when we got out I told her to be on her

---

5   A deep emotional state of melancholic longing and desire
    for something or someone that is absent. It often includes a
    psychological dimension, a repressed knowledge that the thing
    that is longed for will never be seen or experienced again.

way, chick, this is no life for you, she picked up her things and to this day I've not seen her, sir, she left neither scent nor shadow, only scars sir, many scars of pain and sorrow, they are like stab wounds in my heart, I can't forget her, sir, the only thing worse than hunger is the saudade, I haven't eaten anything since the day before yesterday, the day I killed a man and had sex with a woman for the first time, now she's gone, I remain alone again without a thing, without a father, without a mother, without brothers or sisters, I don't know whether I'm a displaced person, or a refugee, or some other thing, I don't know if I will wake up tomorrow, if today I will have to kill again, if a television will appear, if the green kids will turn up, if the soup wagon will come by, and more than anything, sir, I can't take it any longer, give me just a fiver, sir, I'm dying of hunger, no, sir, don't say no, sir, my girl has gone, my hunger is so bad I'm in pain, all I want to do is cry, but I still have the gun in my hand, sir, for fuck's sake, don't provoke me, did you hear that, don't provoke me, sir, give me just a fiver, just a fiver, that's all sir.

The Portuguese Women Are Coming

RTP International (RTPi) interrupted its regular programming to go live to a demonstration in Terreiro do Paço in Lisbon. A group of women were demanding that the Portuguese government support their journey to Angola to rescue their husbands from the sinful clutches of the Angolan black and mixed-race women. The wives in Lisbon believed that their husbands in Angola had been seduced with powders and charms which had turned them into simple vegetables, completely drained of their historical vigor as heirs of Viriato, without any sauce and even less sap or pith.

Although, officially, cannibalism has already been abolished in the African continent, the demonstrators were not ruling out the hypothesis that these perfidious Angolan women might also have eaten the men, and not metaphorically. This gave the protesters the legitimacy they needed to not only demand the immediate intervention of the Portuguese authorities but also that of the United Nations and other actors in the international community, such as the Anglo-American coalition that had recently freed the world from the fantastic threat known as Saddam Hussein. What was happening in Angola, with their husbands (or ex-husbands, who could be sure?) was an authentic genocide that had to be stopped immediately.

The same group now demonstrating in Terreiro do Paço in the heart of the Portuguese capital, had a few months earlier, in the simple city of Bragança in northern Portugal, protested in defense of the sacred stability of the institution of intra-Portuguese marriage. As RTPi had reported at the time, Bragança had been invaded by a crowd of spurious and shameless Brazilian women, whose sole purpose was to steal husbands from the legitimate stock of Portuguese women. As a result, the divorce rate in the locality had shot up since the arrival of these Brazilians, who, mysteriously, could only be seen at night in the local nightclubs and cabarets.

In fact, a man only had to enter one of those dens of iniquity once to see him return home and immediately ask for a divorce from his old wife of many years. The energetic intervention of these women, as the legitimate heirs of the Baker of Aljubarrota, was therefore necessary to restore the law once again. The Bragança City Council promptly intervened and ordered the immediate closure of all night clubs and cabarets, but they reopened a few days later with more palatable names and as cultural and recreational centers. The Brazilians, in turn, changed their nationality.

Now, the attention of these brave women was, in all justice and opportunity, focused on Angola. Indeed, the news that arrived every day from Portugal's former crown jewel in Africa was not only disturbing, but quite terrifying. It was not just the effects of war, the economic backwardness, the dramatic increase in AIDS cases or the widespread corruption among its leaders: if those were the only issues, the Angolans would have dealt with it. However, the problem was something else, and if strategic measures were not taken, it could even put Portugal's national security at risk: the Portuguese men, who had gone to Angola to help the country resolve the problems its very own natives could not, were the targets of a well-woven plot, which could stop them ever setting foot on Portuguese soil again. The operation started in Luanda's airport, where the men were greeted by battalions of black and mixed-race women, who took them to unknown locations. When the men reappeared, they no longer smelt of dirty socks, and they brushed their teeth every day. As if that were not enough, they also danced the semba, the kizomba, the kuduro and the tarrachinha. They had, therefore, been completely tropicalized.

"Fuck!" Joaquim Manuel da Silva could not help but cry out after hearing the RTPi news report. More than amazed, he was literally in panic. He looked to his side, where, sitting in naked splendor, was Zinga Cristina, the beautiful black Angolan he had recently discovered in the

Paradise Club. She was just eighteen years old with eyes so deep they enclosed the wisdom of the whole world, and dark skin as smooth as velvet. But what he saw instead was the image of Maria das Dores, his fat, grey wife with her permanent frown, the woman he had left in Montemor-o-Novo.

Now what? From that moment, the question would hammer in his head.

To be fair, I should say that at this time, he still met all the obligations he had agreed with Zinga Cristina, because the legacy of Viriato and other brave ancestors still ran in his veins. But for the beautiful Angolan, Zinga, there was nothing extraordinary about that. This Portuguese guy had a lot to learn.

Facts, however, do not always happen as predicted or imagined. So, the next day, Joaquim did not appear to take Zinga Cristina to the hairdresser, nor, later, to take her to school. Nor did he answer the numerous calls she made to him on her mobile phone. She also sent several messages through Pedro, the friend who was with him at the Paradise Club, but none of them, as she said, sent any "feedback." It is perfectly understandable therefore that his disappearance and mute silence were interpreted by her in a certain way, and provoked, on her part, a series of verbal responses that don't need to be mentioned.

If the night before, she had paid attention to the RTPi report, she would perhaps have understood what was happening to her new Portuguese boyfriend. But she only watched the soap operas on Globo[6], which, to be fair, are less fanciful than the Portuguese media reports about Angola.

What happened was that Joaquim Manuel da Silva, who had been terribly upset by the story he'd seen the evening before, left early in the morning for the Portuguese Consulate in Luanda, to ask the official if by any chance he knew anything about the arrival of a group of Portuguese women who were coming to Angola in search of their husbands. He asked the question, suddenly and breathlessly without the slightest hesitation.

Caught by surprise, the official took several seconds to answer.

"What! Women? Which women? Where are their husbands?" he began, trying to regain some calm in order to articulate a proper answer. The truth, however, was that he had no idea what this man, looking like a wide-eyed lunatic, was talking about.

Joaquim understood. "Okay," he said, "okay. I must have made a mistake."

But he didn't give up. He called all his Portuguese friends and, unable to hide his anxiety, asked them if they had watched the RTPi report about the Portuguese expeditionaries who, for the sake of the integrity of the Portuguese family, were getting ready to invade Angola. And perhaps they would be preceded, as in the so-called era of the discoverers—although the reasons were

---

6   A Brazilian television station

different then—by some well-intentioned missionary. Unfortunately, none of his countrymen had seen anything. Some were talking about the last Benfica-Sporting match, whilst sipping beer at Trapalhões; others were driving through the streets trying to attract the attention of any young student looking for a lift. Most of them thought his question was completely weird.

That night, Joaquim Manuel da Silva thought he had found some light at the end of the tunnel, when Miguel, whose wife had come with him from Portugal two years ago, told him that she had once confided in him that her friends had advised her—when he decided to go to work in Angola—to accompany him or she would risk being replaced by some Angolan woman. Laughing, Miguel told him that his wife's friends strongly believed that the Angolan women have some special secret that, in their words, enchants all white men they take to bed. But Miguel had no more details than that. And it certainly wasn't advisable to put any questions on the matter to his wife herself, in case she belonged to the group of protesters from the Terreiro do Paço. Joaquim was deeply downhearted.

For a week, he searched the web trying to find something more about the new bakers of Aljubarrota, but he found nothing. He phoned all his friends in Montemor-o-Novo, but none of them could help him either. The oddest thing, however, was that he saw no other media reports about the matter, and nobody else—at least of those he spoke to—had seen the original report on RTPi. Perhaps it was their scoop and, being so extraordinary, no other media outlet had dared to quote from it.

Joaquim Manuel da Silva was so uneasy that, during this entire period, he had no more contact with Zinga Cristina. So he did not know, naturally, that she had met an Italian who had promised to take her to Rome—the author does not know if she accepted this offer or not. A doubt, however, relentlessly punished the mind of her Portuguese ex-boyfriend: how could Maria das Dores have learned that he had met Zinga, just two weeks after his arrival in Angola, where he had gone to become the head chef in a Japanese restaurant that was soon to open in Luanda?

He decided, therefore, to get it all out in the open. Since, from so far away, he obviously couldn't learn much about the Portuguese expeditionaries, which Maria das Dores certainly would have supported—"I'll cut my balls off if she hasn't!" he said, as radically as a man can say—he resolved to travel to Montemor-o-Novo to prevent the women from embarking on their ridiculous adventure.

That was the last thing he should have done.

When he arrived at Montemor-o-Novo, without telling anyone about his arrival, it was already late at night. Therefore, you could only blame him for using his keys and entering the house as quietly as he could to avoid waking up Maria das Dores. What he found was his friend, Antero, on top of her, the pair of them grunting and snorting like two pigs. But Joaquim Manuel da Silva was a peaceful man, so all he did was ask himself:

"And now what? Do I shoot myself in the head or go back to Angola?"

If this story has a bloody ending, it's not my fault.

A Canine Story

Any self-respecting rich man, old or young, must own at least three things (in addition to masses of cash, of course): a dog, a personal guard and a lover. The man in this particular story had the guard, and the lover, but not the dog. He absolutely refused to have any pet in his official home (as he called the house where he lived with his wife and three children) or in the apartment he had recently organized for his lover. In the case of the latter, she had insisted on a pet, even threatening to have a fit if he didn't buy her one, but she soon calmed down when he told her that if she didn't stop causing such mayhem, he would stop paying her bills. He certainly had never read anything by José Cardoso Pires and therefore could not have known what happened, in one of the most disturbing short stories by the Portuguese writer, to a woman who stayed for days and days at home with her German Shepherd dog. Nevertheless, perhaps it was intuition that made him say, so decisively:

"Don't you dare think that I'm like one of those old guys coming out of the bush who's never seen a woman in his life and accepts everything she says or wants! With me, things don't work like that, you hear? I'm already footing all your bills. I've already sorted you out with a home, and I've even promised you a small used car so that you can learn how to drive—but what fantasy is this now, to have a dog in such a tiny apartment! Fuck, it would be trying to bite me whenever I came home in the early hours!"

These, and other reasons, were why Sousa—a friend of his since those youthful times before independence, when they used to play football in the Indigenous Neighborhood and could not have begun to imagine the extraordinary paths their lives would later follow—used to say that he wasn't rich, but merely moneyed. Sousa, himself was a complete bore and as sly as they come. Shortly before the Carnation Revolution in Portugal, he'd managed to leave the country, intending, as he confided to his friends, to join the liberation struggle. The truth, however, was that Sousa went to stay in Paris, where he lived the good life, getting laid with some old woman who sustained him for several years until her (frankly, predictable) death. A few months after the old bird's demise, when he had no more francs in his pocket, Sousa returned to Luanda, calling himself a "cultural producer", a profession seen by everyone as rather obscure and esoteric. He was, at the same time, an expert in aphorisms. "Wine is not to drink but to get drunk on," he would say, for example.

But Sousa didn't know what he was talking about. The life of his old friend from the Indigenous Neighborhood had made several turns of more than 360 degrees. The most recent turn was a few months back when he was appointed to the board of the state-owned oil company, and this had catapulted him into the restricted and closed circle of the country leaders. In contrast to the painful remarks made by this circle's numerous detractors— usually during funerals and Saturday lunch parties—given that Angola was an oil-producer who else was there to take charge of its destiny?

"Even the Americans," he used to say, "know that they have to get along with us. In 2007, they'll be importing more oil from Angola than from Kuwait!"

To be candid, he did not really have the brains to become a member of any bloody board, least of all of the company where they put him, but an extraordinary stroke of luck made possible what many still find unbelievable. How it happened was that one day he was getting his calluses treated when he bumped into an old friend he had not seen since independence and who had become one of the most influential people in the country. They exchanged cards and promised to meet again as soon as possible, which meant, that they would probably not see each other again. However, in this case, events developed more swiftly and unusually than anyone of sound mind could possibly imagine. Just two weeks after, he got a call from the old friend.

"I'm calling to tell you that I will be nominating you to join the board of a new association that we will be establishing soon.

Being one of us and, furthermore, being experienced in this field, I believe your name will be easily approved. Will you accept?"

Of course, he knew he had no experience of this kind whatsoever. In the foreign oil company where he had been employed for the last three years, he had never held a position of real responsibility at all. He was a technician, not even an engineer. Yet, he accepted, even though he had never read Paul Auster either, and deep inside he knew that life was made up of more details and chances than was imagined in the vain rationalism and Judeo-Christian moralism with which the West attempts to stain our thoroughly Bantu nature. And so, just like that, he became a member of the board of that "corporation of the future", as he termed it when he told his wife and children that their lives would soon be changing.

The rest is so predictable, it's not worth recounting.

What should be remembered, however, was that now he had a personal guard and a lover, but not a dog, as he would never accept Marlene's silly idea that in Brazil it is fashionable for women to have little dogs as pets! Marlene and, he remembered now, Sousa too, for fuck's sake! Thinking it over fully, he wondered why he continued to be friends with Sousa, who had questioned his new appointment to the board during the dinner to celebrate the appointment.

"Member of the board? What do you know about being a board member of an oil company?" Sousa had asked before vomiting heavily in the kitchen, which he was naturally entitled to enter being a close friend of the family.

Soon enough when it became obvious just how much his life had improved, Sousa would often tell him that he hadn't become anything more than a mere moneyed guy since he had neither expected or prepared to be suddenly so wealthy. Indeed, one of the arguments Sousa used to corroborate his theory was that his friend never even considered offering a puppy—a terrier, for example, would have been a good choice—to his lover, thereby confirming his lack of culture and refinement, and that he had not shed his uncouth nature. Strangely, however, he did not notice the hidden message in these words and continued to treat Sousa just as he always had during the good old days in the Indigenous Neighborhood.

And this is why this story ends in a completely unpredictable way, at least as far as I'm concerned. It so happened that he had to travel to London, to address his long-lasting health problem, his calluses. Afterwards, he went on to Lisbon, where his children were pursuing their studies and where his wife would meet them so they could all be together, which had not been the case since the previous Christmas. In total, he was out of the country for about a month. For sure, Marlene must have been feeling very lonely during this period, and she would also have been having a hard time solving certain practical issues such as paying her water and energy bills, and telephoning the company that normally delivered gas to her flat. Nowadays, Sousa was, in all truth, his only real friend, since his appointment with the state oil company, which had led him to discover an otherwise hidden feature among most of his old friends: envy. Therefore, nothing could have been more normal, during his absence, than for him to ask Sousa to help Marlene.

A month or so later, on his return from Lisbon, he went straight to Marlene's apartment (his wife, I should explain, was spending a few more days in Portugal) where he was amazed to discover that his key did not fit in the lock. So, under the circumstances, he rang the bell. The door opened, with the safety chain still hooked, and Marlene's face appeared in the crack of the door. Yes, Marlene, the lover he had found for himself at the very first reception he attended after being appointed to his new post. Perhaps it was his fatigue from the long flight that made him not to immediately recognize his lover's face nor understand her brutal and abrupt words:

"What do you want, you fucking moron? Go away! Get away from my life! Go to your wife and pretend that you never met me!"

Even now, he still cannot forget all the tiny details of that moment: in the living room, he could see Sousa sitting on the sofa, cross-legged, with a terrier puppy on his lap, cuddling its little head and looking as relaxed and delighted as you can imagine.

Sheesh

Mister X. Readers may pronounce this name the Portuguese way—sheesh—or the English way (as a matter of modesty, I refuse to spell out the English pronunciation of this tiny and mysterious letter because it would be a black mark against my CV). Where I wrote "modesty," you may read, if you wish, "national-linguistic pride," but I hope no traditionalist wastes any time reading my stories because then I won't have to be reminded that Portuguese is the colonial language and that the most patriotic way to spell the original African languages is Anglo-Saxon. For, despite my dislike of trouble—in contrast to most Angolans—I would have to respond that we, the Caluandas[7] at any rate, have already nationalized the language of Viriato, Diogo Cão, and others like them, if you know what I mean.

But it is not because of this subject that I have called you here.

---

7   Someone from the Angolan city of Luanda

Before moving on to the great revelation I have in store for you—don't mind my immodesty—I must inform you that to safeguard the narrator's intellectual integrity (don't laugh, I beg you!), whichever option you've chosen regarding the pronunciation of the name mentioned above, you are only allowed to know the name: Mister X. No other identification will be put forward, much less, those details that are utterly useless in this uncharacteristic but global abyss that is the world today, such as ancestry, origins, nationality and even distinguishing marks. In an age of imploding boundaries and stolen patents, of general eclecticism, unknown compounds, of cell transfusion and cloning, only those who are poor in spirit can afford to lose time and energy on the grotesque attempt to remain glued to identities that are fixed and closed, even to themselves. For the record—and above all, to protect the author's image among his neighbors—the narrator takes full and complete responsibility for the absurd reflections just made. So let's move on.

Mister X had a habit that may seem strange today, though it was perfectly normal and even common back then and in the context in which the facts of this story took place: he only read the obituary pages of the daily newspaper, *Jornal de Angola*. While we have time, we can share with you, dear readers, some of the motives for this now recognized and informative interest which, having nurtured it, had become, from the outset, deeply rooted in his all-embracing character. In effect, these obituary pages fulfilled a primary function—to name those who had passed away, thereby enabling relatives, friends, and acquaintances of the deceased to put in an appearance at the funeral, the seventh day mass, and the komba, the rituals that, among other things, offered a propitious occasion for people to get together, having not seen each other for a long time, and also where they could eat and drink at will. At the same time, they also served a series of secondary functions whose importance you might be able to understand from what follows.

The funereal notices published in the *Jornal de Angola* were a precious way of learning, for example, whether the deceased had, during his or her lifetime, observed the sort of safe sexual practices demanded in present times (so, to say that a man or a woman passed away due to "a long-term illness" usually meant that death had been caused by the awful HIV virus or AIDS, though, sometimes, noises would be made during the communication process such that, in the end, the deceased could equally have died from cancer). Some of the notices were really formal accusations, albeit disguised ones, against certain institutions, as was the case with the warnings announcing someone's death "by assassination"—with no mention of the perpetrator of the deed since the public would already know who the scoundrel was. Nevertheless, don't think I'm going to reveal who it was: I don't want to turn into a funereal notice in any newspaper.

Another use for the obituaries in *Jornal de Angola* was to know how the deceased (in this case, only those of the male sex) had been able to manage a double-life, and sometimes a triple-life or even more, as the majority of men do regardless of whether they admit to it or not (to do justice to my feminist readers, I must say that, in those times, as always, there were also women who had led parallel lives, although the press tended not to mention them, which only goes to show just how competent these women were). Taking note of this, therefore, despite the lack of reliable data, only the one known as "the first" (nearly always, merely a bureaucratic classification...) would, in the great majority of cases, shoulder the public notice about the death of her respective spouse, even though she had had to share him with one or even more women. But there were some cases in which either the first or the second took charge of the public notice, communicating the passing of the man whom they had shared, peacefully or not. Less commonly, the first and the second would publish—both on their behalf and that of all the children—a single funereal notice, and this, for Mister X, who had known neither wife nor children, was the height of happiness. At this point, the narrator's explanations about the enormous advantages of the obituary pages in *Jornal de Angola* shall cease before revealing all their weaknesses to the readers too.

The only thing I wish to add is that nobody knows which of the advantages or uses detailed above were at the root of Mister X's genuine fixation with the obituary pages in the mentioned newspaper. Almost certainly, all of them interested him to a certain extent, but could it have been that he established some sort of hierarchy among them? The fact is, as I have already said (after all, redundancy is one of the conditions for the efficiency of communication), that he only read those particular pages. He refused even to glance at the cover. In fact, he would flee from it as the devil allegedly flees from the cross: as soon as he picked up the newspaper, he would fold over the cover and desperately scramble for the last pages where the obituaries were lined up, usually with a photo of the deceased above the text giving the impression, for whoever looked at these pages globally, as he did, of tombs arranged in a graveyard in an orderly fashion.

The technique developed by Mister X—quite empirically, let me tell you—in which he would begin by taking a quick and generalized glance of the relevant pages, had an extremely simple goal, but which immediately enabled one to grasp the generous nature of this man who, nevertheless, had an unexpected and unjust destiny. What was at stake was to recognize, in one of the photographs, a family member, no matter how distant, or a friend, even one he'd fallen out with, or simply someone with whom he was acquainted, no matter how ill-considered that was, to start a detailed reading of these sought-after pages of *Jornal de Angola*. When he did not recognize a face, he would invariably start reading from left to right and from top to bottom, as our visual culture demands. Naturally, I am not yet going to reveal the concrete fate reserved for Mister X by the gods, even if nothing, theoretically speaking, is stopping me from doing so. Indeed, this narrative, contrary to what it may appear to be, is not a detective story whose secrets are only revealed at the very end. On the other hand—and given that I have already had the opportunity to read somewhere that starting a story at the end is thought to be a very good post-modern technique or, at least, can in itself lend the text some glamour—the fact is that I, myself, still don't know Mister X's real and effective fate, despite the fact, I confess, that I have already dared to start sketching it inside my head. But if in life we don't always achieve what we want, what can we expect from literature?

By the way, I must state that the technique developed by Mister X did not always produce the results he hoped for. Sometimes, while he was making that first panoramic observation of the obituary pages of the *Jornal de Angola* (there were between two to four pages a day, depending upon the number of dead), he did not discover anyone he knew (while they had been un-dead, of course), neither directly related nor merely someone he recognized as a passer-by in the street. However, when he was engaged in the second and more detailed reading, he would come across someone he knew in a photo dating back ten, twenty, or even thirty years. This would profoundly exasperate him. What was the reason behind this strategy of camouflage which was adopted by the family members of so many of the deceased? Mister X never found an answer to this distressing question, and the strain would haunt him right up to his own abrupt ending. As far as I am concerned, I cannot help him either, even posthumously, but I hope that, wherever he is, he will forgive my incompetence.

In the meantime, and although I never managed to discover the reason, Mister X was never despondent. He retaliated with passion against the authors of this wickedness. His first response was to fail to turn up at the funerals, the memorials, the wakes, the kombas and all the other events designed to, as it is said, commit the souls of the departed. The day immediately following the memorial, after the sweeping of the ashes (which, for sure, my Icelandic and Mongolian readers will not know that this takes place thirty days after someone's death), he would wear his best attire and go to the home of the deceased, whereupon he would enter swiftly and tenderly and ask if the aforementioned person was there because he would like to invite him to share a few beers. As I have never been present during these visits, I cannot tell you exactly what would happen, but it is not hard to imagine that they were probably pretty stressful situations given the, so to speak, post-burial climate.

The truth is that Mister X brought these provocative visits to an end shortly after, offering no explanation whatsoever. But he did not abandon his desire to revenge those liars who had the notorious habit of deceiving readers of *Jornal de Angola* on matters such as the age of the deceased (this entire expression is his). So whenever he came across one of these cases, he would send a note to the newspaper confirming the death of the dead person in question, but including a most intriguing and enticing headline, disclosing maybe a certain journalistic feeling (or irresponsibility) on his part: THE DECEASED WANTS HIS FACE BACK. In the text, Mister X would fiercely and rudely attack the relatives of the deceased for daring to publish, in the previous day's edition, a false photograph of the deceased, which only confirmed—as if this was necessary—the anomie that characterizes current times. For quite some time—a period which, given the empire of speed in which we live, is hard to measure—he devoted himself to this strange hobby, which he considered to be a completely irremediable civic duty from which he could not escape.

One day, something snapped inside his head. In other words, he had a brainwave. These two expressions, which, at first sight, are so deplorably and miserably commonplace, nevertheless, have a philosophical depth to which no one pays enough attention. Mister X, himself, was amazed, and asked himself the question that all human beings ask when they become aware of their utter ignorance about these things to which they are closest (people included): WHY DIDN'T I THINK OF THIS SOONER? What happened then, whether you believe it or not, was that Mister X—thanks to his continuous and obsessive pondering of the reasons why some people illustrate the obituary notices of their loved ones with extremely outdated photos in such a way that the deceased will only be recognized by the very few who enjoy an outstanding visual memory, which unfortunately was certainly not the case for him—was driven by one of those oblique lines of thought that is so peculiar to the human mind and which led him, finally, to reach the frightening formulation of mankind's largest and most persistent existential question: WHO ARE WE?

In reality, if certain people had not hesitated from using outdated photographs to confirm the physical disappearance of others to whom they were linked through special ties and, therefore, unless proved otherwise, having no reason to commit unfriendly acts against them, especially when they had become—as certified by materialist logic—thoroughly harmless beings, there was only one conclusion: *identity is the color of a donkey running away.* Mister X recalled that this sentence was written by some Angolan poet, which reinforced his natural sympathy towards poets and Angolan people too. As far as he was concerned, he would not hesitate to sign up to the above-mentioned sentence.

Mister X thus decided to stop worrying about that which he had previously considered a notorious method of camouflage used by the relatives of certain dead people, for reasons that neither he nor the narrator, and even less so the readers, had or would ever come to know. He, therefore, stopped writing to *Jornal de Angola* to mercilessly attack these relatives. But don't think that he stopped reading the obituary pages of the newspaper. He simply found a new ambition. Now, he wouldn't simply try to learn which relative, friend, or acquaintance had parted from this world for another, to attend the customary rites of passage, including the more or less copious kombas, nor was he compelled any longer by any, let's say, detective nose driving him forward to expose those liars who were trying to cover up the true or, at least, the latest face of the departed, in order to submit them to his fierce and natural sense of justice. Furthermore, his cruel attraction to the obituary pages of the mentioned newspaper was not stimulated by any morbid curiosity to uncover the immoral secrets that the deceased had managed to conceal while still alive. Mister X's reasons were much more unusual than that.

His goal, now, was nothing more and nothing less than to appropriate the identities of some of these men and even women, whose deaths had definitely been announced in the two to four pages of *Jornal de Angola*, for which he waited anxiously every morning. Thus, each day, he would select one of them, sometimes making compositions using elements from others that, for some obscure reason, pleased him, and he would make a new name using select elements. *If the dead can have several faces* (and already, various biographies, according to the biographer), *why can't I have several names?* Mister X asked himself.

With these new selections—that changed every day—in his pocket, he entered a new and higher phase of existence, according to his own assessment. The first precaution he took was to stop using his identity card, an object that had become useless now that he had discovered that a face and an identity have nothing to do with each other. Besides, in those days, an identity card demanded from citizens a pre-historic detail, which he abhorred: "race" (the quotation marks are his, the narrator's, and the author's). So he decided to keep his inside a drawer so that an archaeologist might eventually find it, several centuries later, and have it classified as a sample of how human stupidity materialized in a particular time and place. Next, he started spreading terror, as we call it, around the city (with the exception of the Jacobin resonances of this expression, which were formulated by an independent newspaper at the time) in the name of all the multiple identities that he had decided to adopt, which may well explain the unusual end he would eventually meet.

In those days the spaces for civic expression were indeed few and limited, but Mister X courageously managed to occupy them all. His strategy was a simple one: every day he would send a letter to an institution whose mandate was to care for citizens. In each letter, he would expose a problem or a situation, submitting a denunciation, a complaint, or a claim, and would make a demand or suggest a solution, signing each letter with a different name. For him, no subject was too small or insignificant. Equally, he did not let any institution off the hook. He would write daily to the president, the parliament, the government, the armed forces, the chairmen of the boards, the judges, the press, the businessmen, the churches, the scholars' associations, the NGOs, the winners of beauty contests, as well as to the great chiefs, the average chiefs and even the little ones, both real and fake. Mister X's civic-epistolary fury spared no one, not even the many parallel committees, established in those strange times, to perform tasks that should have been performed by the institutions foreseen in the flowcharts of the State.

As you might easily predict, Mister X could only meet with an end that matched his biography. One day, he was finishing one of his many letters when, without asking permission, a group of assorted individuals entered his home. They were all quite short and had a provocative air about them and, having no index fingers, approached him pointing their little fingers. *Usurper!* they shouted. *Usurper!* Apoplectic, they demanded to see his identity card immediately. But, as has been explained already, Mister X did not have such a card. So, he was taken away by these strangers, whom the neighbors could not identify beyond the few who suggested they were policemen and others who suggested they were journalists because they had tape-recorders in their hands and were poorly-dressed, and a few others who said they were priests or, due to their angelic looks, members of some cult at the very least. To add to the confusion, a few of them were seen getting out of luxurious cars, similar to those owned by members of parliament, and others were wearing traditional lucky charms over their impeccable western outfits as if they were post-modern traditional chiefs. Others seemed to represent some foreign NGO because not only did they have blond hair, but they were also wearing brand new jeans, fashionable trainers, and had flat bottoms.

In any case, since the beginning of this story, Mister

X has been destined to disappear. I, myself, as the narrator, have left several clues in this sense, daring myself (unwisely, I confess) to predict his unjust and inglorious end. His neighbors are certain, meanwhile, that he has disappeared, yes, although he was not taken away by any strangers. According to what they say, when Mister X was being pushed into one of the cars, all the cell phones of the aforementioned strangers began to ring loudly at the same time, and they were seen changing color as well as making expansive gestures and looking at each other with their eyes wide open as if they were about to pop out of their sockets. Without breathing a word, they made a sign at Mister X to go back into his home, leaving them to get back into their cars and simply leave. At that very moment, a newspaper vendor was passing by with *Jornal de Angola*. Mister X purchased a copy, but he did not go into his house: he disappeared but in a very different way.

The narrator would be grateful, therefore, for any news of Mister X, to enable him end this story.

The Secret

This story happened in Haifa. I have never been to Haifa, but I've always wanted to write a story that takes place in the city. Likewise, I will not die without writing a story located in Mexico City, Venice, Salvador, Kathmandu, and New York. The (almost) Shakespearean question that plays havoc with me when I am caught up in these delights, is whether the guardians of patriotic integrity in the national literature will cease considering me an Angolan author for daring to locate my tales in spurious, exogenous environments instead of restricting myself to local Bantu landscapes.

Thus, I remember—with a shock no doubt identical to that experienced by those condemned to be roasted in the medieval bonfires of the Inquisition—that the playwright José Mena Abrantes was accused of not being Angolan for writing a play called *The King's Orphan*. It was about the peripeteia of a Portuguese girl, who was part of a group of white teenagers sent to Angola in the seventeenth century by the king of Portugal. The girls were to marry the settlers before they took up with native women and contributed—as Viriato da Cruz has said, albeit in another context—to the darkening of the race. *Yaka*, one of the best novels by the celebrated author Pepetela, was also considered a colonial novel because the central characters were members of a settler family in Benguela.

More extraordinary, in both cases, is that the accusers were well-known opponents of the country's governing party, which they considered to be anti-democratic and dictatorial. Thus, they proved that if not subjected to a permanent process of questioning and evaluation, even the most well-intentioned and generous ideologies— those formulated to function as forces of consciousness, mobilization, and most of all, human transformation— run the risk of becoming instruments for the exclusion of others and even bloody repression and attempted annihilation. This is the reason oppressed people tend to mimic their oppressors and why revolutionaries become conservative or even counter-revolutionaries. The contemporary world is not, therefore, a very pleasant place, but it is the place in which we are fated to live.

As you have surely gathered, I'm particularly pessimistic today. I have just connected to the internet and I am reading a story in a Colombian newspaper about a woman in Haifa, who managed to hide her deafness from her husband for exactly twenty-five years. In all honesty, I do not know which is the more scandalous: the self-proclaimed democrats, who hide within themselves their barely-disguised autocratic and exclusionary tendencies which come out of their mouths at the first opportunity, or this woman, who, for exactly a quarter of a century, was able to conceal such a ridiculous and distressing secret from her own spouse, the man with whom she supposedly shared all the good and bad things in her life. Will this be, after all, the dilemma for post-modern literature— whether one should take a stand on the big questions facing mankind, or whether one should worry about the stories of the day-to-day existence of the men and women who live on our planet?

The truth is that, far away from this duplicitous mess, there was a woman, who lived in the city of Haifa and who concealed from her husband her very poor hearing for twenty-five years. As we know, Haifa is in the so-called Middle East, one of the most explosive regions in the world, to use the journalese. To contrast with current advice, or the tendency of all the best-selling authors, prior to writing this story, I did not have time to conduct any research. As such, I imagine Haifa to be a white city as well as a secular one (with all the implications that the word carries), a city that is totally covered in the dust that was originally sand that came from the nearby desert. Not having forgotten, meanwhile, the input of a certain useless culture that follows us through life, I can also imagine men and women walking through the streets in long white outfits and in the case of the women, with veils covering their faces. Cars, mostly old ones but a few modern ones too, are moving sluggishly through the city. If you are lucky, you can still see a few donkeys, evoking memories of those old times that are vanishing so relentlessly each day. Confirming the unceasing intensity of the disappearance of those times, Haifa has a new part too, an area that is developing far from the port to which the city has traditionally been identified.

Whether a city like this exists or not, the first question we can ask, having—at last!—reached the end of the beginning of the story, is the reason for the woman's deafness. Was she born with this defect? Apparently not, since she could speak normally with other people, as we shall learn before this story's end. Another hypothesis, maybe a more plausible one, is that she was among the many victims of the war that has, for centuries, afflicted the region. Most likely, she became deaf, at least partially, due to the detonation of some deadly device exploding close to the place where she was hiding, in one of those daily battles, insane and inexplicable (at least for me, living so far away from the region), that continue to shake the Middle East. The words that I have just used to classify the fighting in the region may seem unjust, at least when told by someone who has experienced four decades of war during the twentieth and twenty-first centuries, but the truth is that the human tendency to gaze only at another's buttocks is as unsolvable a mystery as the origin of the Haifa woman's deafness.

The second question to ask is the following: why did this woman conceal her deafness from her husband? Whatever the culture of the author may be (and however useless), among the different religions fighting with one another in the Middle East there is not known to be any taboo (the traditionalists among you may read kijila) against the physical impossibility of hearing the daily hubbub of the world. Moreover, the Colombian newspaper where I first read this story did not state whether her husband had any kind of anger towards or phobia of deafness, which proves that, contrary to what its practitioners claim, journalism is not the most comprehensive, precise, or exact (let's not even mention objective!) form of communication. Once again, therefore, it is literature that is called upon to save mankind, or at least to save its readers.

The author is of the firm belief that the husband nurtured a secret joy for the fact that his wife could not hear a single noise. However, do not rush into thinking of him as a monster because the truth is that he loved his wife just as she was. The biggest hypocrites might say this meant nothing since, in addition to love being a highly plastic emotion not only favorable to all sorts of uses but also to all sorts of justifications and excuses, the concept of truth is equally highly debatable, at least since the Greeks (so we are told) invented philosophy with at least five strands. It is said that one of these strands is close to the truth of the rabid shamelessness of the cynics.

Thus, the husband could have been completely at ease with his wife's deafness for, let us say, opportunistic reasons since a spouse who is unable to hear offers certain advantages for the other after all. These advantages can be unfolded almost infinitely. For example, just imagine him being able to snore at all times without ever facing the recrimination of his wife. Or, in bed, swapping her name for that of his mistress without running any risk whatsoever of being thrown out of the room, or having to divorce or even die. And what about the delicious pleasure of producing certain eschatological noises without being pushed out of bed, or having to listen to insults from his wife? Not to mention the supreme joy of never again having to repeat relentless vows and worn-out promises of love simply because she can't be bothered to listen to them...

Last but not least, we can even imagine something which is a bit like the icing on the cake: in addition to all the above-mentioned advantages, this woman's deafness would have made it impossible for her to hear any of the precious information reported by her friends about her husband's extra-marital affairs. Indeed, I have heard that after the marital brainstorming that she carried out with her friends (to call them "gossip sessions" would be too prosaic), she remained oddly calm and serene. She did not shout and curse, she did not pull out her hair, strip off her veil, nor cry and throw herself to the floor. Considering that human beings usually tend to analyze others according to stereotypes, many might attribute her behavior to some cultural disposition (I've already said that this story happened in Haifa, but these cultural explanations can, in truth, be found where one least expects them), yet in this case, the cause was not that complex, at least sociologically: she did not hear any of the accusations—by which I mean absolutely none—that her friends told her so vehemently and with such conviction.

It is not, therefore, out of stubbornness that I feel suspicious of this woman's husband, who, indeed, I have never met. For him, his wife's deafness should have been like heaven on earth. He was living, have no doubt, in some kind of nirvana. It would have been different if instead of his wife concealing her deafness from him, she was concealing the fact she did not feel any pleasure, or that she had a lover, or that she was a lesbian. Men, so we say, usually lose control when they learn about these kinds of secrets. And to be fair, this is not only the case in Haifa; on the contrary, it happens in the best families and in the best civilizations. What we can say, in these cases, is that the degree of male rage varies according to the three mentioned situations, although, strangely, the feeling might be the same: everyone who experiences it feels unquestionably betrayed. "Cuckolds" is, in truth, the right word. Cuckolds in themselves, in the first case; cuckolds of any son of a bitch, in the second; and in the third and final case and perhaps most despicable of all, "cuckolds of a cow" as a certain misogynistic Angolan writer used to say.

Be that as it may, as far as I can work out, this man has no reason to complain. Apparently, he was able to give his wife not fictitious but real orgasms; she did not have a lover (either that, or she had concealed him as well as she had concealed her deafness for the past twenty-five years); and lastly, she had not "gone over to the opposition," as the saying has come to be known since the political system opened up in Angola, and not without a slight and tolerant irony, referring to someone who has, openly or not, opted for homosexuality. What I could not find out was whether an analogous expression is used in Haifa, though I am sure it must exist. One question remains, however: if they really were without any marital problems, why did the woman conceal her deafness for so long? I am sorry to confess that, despite my best efforts, I have not been able to clear this up.

Before my readers feel tempted to doubt the investigative capacity of the author, let me attempt to answer the third and final question that must necessarily be asked: how this woman was able to conceal the secret from her husband for such a long time? Not since a certain British diplomat was duped by a Chinese spy, had such a cinematic and (well-disguised) metamorphosis been heard of—otherwise that episode would never have been immortalized on film in *Madame Butterfly*. In sum, how can someone who is deaf pretend for no less than twenty-five years, and without being found out, that she has the same ability as every other mortal to hear the polyphonic noises of the world? How could this extraordinary woman of Haifa, in the early morning, answer her husband's more or less loving farewells? How, in the evening, could she react to his high or low-spirited greetings? How could she know, at the table, that he had asked her for the bread and not the knife, or, in bed, that he just wanted to lie at her side and sleep instead of trying again?

I don't know.

This unusual story received no more than ten short lines in the online edition of the Colombian newspaper where I read it. I must say that when I first heard about it, I felt as if I had been attacked by an overwhelming concern that made me search the internet desperately for more details. But that first story was all I could find. For several days, I searched the principal oracles of our times, such as CNN, the BBC, and Sky News, but it was all in vain. The only thing known is that after twenty-five years, this Haifa woman's husband acknowledged that he had been living with someone unable to hear any noise, not even the faintest, because the mailman had absentmindedly given him a letter from a hearing-aid manufacturer addressed to his wife.

The husband's reaction remains unknown. Could it be that when he opened this curious letter to his wife that he fell to the ground as if struck by lightning? Would he have fled their house, to be lost forever in the desert, fearing that his wife, at the end of the day, knew all about his hairy secrets that he thought he had concealed from her for the last twenty-five years? Or did he take his scimitar from the trunk where he had kept it for so many years, to polish it particularly carefully, while waiting for his wife with a peculiar quietness to his gestures and his eyes as blue as the Haifa sky, as if he had always imagined such a situation?

Nobody knows.

I have begun to believe that one of the most complex

problems facing humankind today is the entropy of communication.

The author is forced to acknowledge his frustration because, after all this, he knows nothing about this case of the woman who concealed her deafness from her own husband for twenty-five years. I do not even know why this story captured my attention in the first place. Possibly because it occurred in Haifa, a remote and foreign city, where I have never been, as I mentioned earlier, and for which reason I am running the risk of being forcefully withdrawn from the select (or, better said, selected) pantheon of national authors. To save my own skin, I only have one solution: to telephone the woman in Haifa.

—*And what do you, a simple Angolan writer, have to do with my life?* replies a voice from the other side of the world.

A Bloody Mystery

Mrs. Magui was far from being, shall we say, a global citizen, since she neither traveled much, nor used cable TV, nor the Internet, but somehow she had the feeling that the world was becoming an increasingly dangerous and insecure place. I cannot say if this perception was down to hearsay since Mrs. Magui—who received practically no visitors at all at her home in downtown Luanda—was not interested in gossiping with her neighbors. The truth of the matter is that she was so bothered by this aforementioned feeling that she began to take special measures whenever she had to go out. For example, she was constantly looking around, abruptly changing direction, walking in circles, and even wearing disguises, some of which were extremely crude, like the blonde wig which made her Angolan cafusa[8] skin look

---

8 Cafusa refers to her skin-colour. In Angola, it is common to describe people in terms of their so-called race. There are five categories, including: white, cabrito (one mixed-race and one white parent), mestiço (two mixed-race parents), cafuso (one mixed-race and one black parent), and black.

even darker. With time, her outings became less and less frequent until, one day, they stopped entirely and Mrs. Magui purely and simply ceased to be seen on the street. Her feelings of fear and insecurity had become completely unbearable.

Fortunately, her goddaughter, Sandrinha, lived with her. If that were not the case, the narrator would probably have had to devise some tragedy to tell the tale of what happened to Mrs. Magui. She had looked after Sandrinha since the day she was born. Sandrinha's mother, who had died during childbirth, was Mrs. Magui's old friend and had invited her to be godmother to her child as soon as she had discovered she was pregnant.

—You have always wished for a child, my friend. Take care of my baby as if she was your own! said Sandrinha's mother on her deathbed.

Given that she did not know who the child's father was, for reasons you will understand a little later, Mrs. Magui had had to take care of Sandrinha from the moment she was born, in the hope that some relative, however distant, would appear at any moment to take the child away. Nobody appeared, however, so Sandrinha became the daughter Mrs. Magui never had.

Mrs. Magui and Sandrinha, who was now fifteen years old, had been living in the apartment for just a year and three months. It is quite unlikely that there is any link between the two facts, but when it is not possible to identify the so-called scientific causes for human phobias, the mind has an odd, if understandable tendency to find apparently absurd justifications and, stranger still, not very reassuring ones, that may nevertheless explain humanity's propensity for depression and suffering. The fact is that Mrs. Magui was certain that she only began to feel fearful of the world exactly one year and three months ago, when she had moved with her goddaughter to that part of the city. Wisely, she did not share her conviction with anybody, which, at the very least, spared her from certain labels or nicknames, which thou (allow me this secular term) may choose as thou please.

At this point in the story, let me provide a brief explanation to avoid anyone jumping to any conclusions. Luanda, a four-hundred-year-old African city, which many confuse with Uganda, is far from being one of the most dangerous and challenging places in the world, as far as urban security is concerned. Just to give you a small example, as they say, I can reveal that in this forgotten city on the Atlantic, one can still enjoy a quick, and more or less, quiet fuck in the car by the sea at two in the morning. I hope, with this sincere and well-intended disclosure, that I am not offending any strong moral principle nor breaking any patriotic secrets of state. Indeed, the risk of being blamed for going too far stops me from proposing that this precious information be used for a major international campaign to promote tourism to the country, starting with the capital, which has got to be one of the most erotic and lecherous cities on the planet, at least according to the narrator who, being more global than Mrs. Magui, can make certain comparisons which allow him to make such a statement.

It is true that, by the time these events took place, most of the buildings and houses in Luanda were protected by good old steel railings, although, strictly speaking, this was, as a matter of fact, no more than an architectural trend of extremely bad taste. Likewise, if anyone wanted to calculate the number of private security guards per meter-squared of the city, there is no doubt he would be amazed by the results of such an exercise. Still, this could be seen as merely typical of the fashions of the nouveau riche, who had suddenly risen to the surface of the national landscape like some kind of weed. It is also true, in the period to which we are referring, that a series of very strange criminal phenomena had started occurring in Luanda, the sort that are only seen on television, for instance, those resulting from the activities of gangs of youths, but which the public never get to hear much about because the parents of these youths are those who enjoy immunity from the law (don't ask me why, because I am but a simple writer, not a social researcher).

Mrs. Magui, therefore, did not have, in principle, good reason to feel unsafe like the inhabitants of the planet's other cities, because in general, Luanda could still be considered a peaceful city, despite the stoic and quite pathetic efforts of Portuguese television to damage its tropical reputation and hospitality. As far as the area where Mrs. Magui and her goddaughter, Sandrinha, had moved to (exactly a year and three months ago), it was a bit quieter than the rest of the city. In fact, the dull monotony of the place was interrupted only once in a while by two ridiculous crimes. One of them happened mostly at the main road junctions whenever the traffic stopped or slowed down, giving just enough time for the fake street peddlers—who wander around before swiftly moving in to lean like Spider-Man on car windows, especially those driven by women—to snatch the golden chains from the necks of the latter, or to distract the driver for long enough to take the bag placed carelessly on the seat, as if waiting for the children of God, who also need to eat. The other crime, which involved stealing cell phones in the middle of the street, targeted young students and girls and was mainly carried out by groups of youths who were just as thirsty for the recent wonders of communication technology as anyone else. No wonder, when every day they are relentlessly bombarded with messages from the prevailing consumerist ideology. Rarefied crimes like this do not deserve to be dealt with by literature, therefore I won't waste any more time describing them. Furthermore, I am fully aware that what the readers want to know is why Mrs. Magui had stopped leaving her house, with this terrible fear of violence.

This mystery, I must say, intrigued all of Mrs. Magui's and Sandrinha's neighbors. Given what they all knew— the terrified look in her eyes whenever she saw a stranger, her habit of walking in circles and around the block, and those occasions when she was seen wearing her blonde wig—they had all, without exception, made up their minds, definitely and irreversibly, about the old maid, who was nearly fifty and who had moved in precisely one year and three months earlier with her sweet and responsible fifteen-year-old goddaughter: she was nuts. In fact, they not only thought that, but they also spoke about it freely inside their homes, in hallways, in the grocery next door, and in the local hairdresser's. Nevertheless, what they wanted to know was the same as what the readers want to know: why?

To resolve this most serious of matters upon which the very equilibrium of the community depended, Mrs. Magui's neighbors used a variety of tactics and strategies. They started with the most obvious: on the pretext of small domestic favors, still used regularly by Angolans, such as a little bit of sugar, a pinch of salt, or two or three chili peppers, they tried to find out more about the inside of her home in the hope of eventually discovering something suspicious. This rather too obvious strategy failed because Mrs. Magui never left them unattended, preferring instead to pass every little thing through the railings, which were kept closed at all times. Following this, they tried waiting outside her home for those few minutes each morning when she came out to sweep the entrance. They would attempt to engage her in every kind of chit-chat, be it about the weather, the price of goods in the shops, the government, and all sorts of other similar themes, but she simply wouldn't respond to anyone— apart from one day when, foolishly, someone asked her about the blonde wig. The answer they received could not have astounded them more:

—*So, you think I'm some kind of a whore?*

The neighbors' final attempt to find out why Mrs. Magui, with her fear of violence and insecurity, had given up leaving her home, involved approaching her goddaughter. They had gained a very favorable impression of Sandrinha thanks to her sympathetic and peaceful appearance, as well as the way she behaved towards everybody. This impression was consolidated when they learned she had become her godmother's true supporter, in so far as, from the first day Mrs. Magui had decided to stay at home, Sandrinha had become the only link connecting this shrunken human microcosm (that was the two women) to the outside world. To be sure, Sandrinha did not allow herself to become contaminated by her godmother's anxiety and, apparently, took control of their home. She was doing all the shopping, throwing the trash into the container two blocks away, buying the daily newspapers, and even taking part in the neighborhood committee meetings. At the same time, though her godmother wouldn't drive her anymore, Sandrinha continued to attend her classes on the other side of town, leaving the house much earlier each day to catch the bus. The neighbors began, genuinely and sincerely, to admire her.

What was most impressive was that Sandrinha did not mind doing everything. She did not feel burdened by her lot. She was as light and cheerful as when she had first arrived. No shadow darkened her adolescent eyes. She would always greet elderly people respectfully, and always have a joke or a loving word for the youngest. She, however, maintained her distance from the young men (and the older ones) who, naturally, wanted to get a little closer. Mrs. Albertina, the building's oldest resident, always advised Sandrinha on the best way to keep the young boys away, as well as the shameless and abusive old men. But she did not understand why Sandrinha started sobbing before plunging into silence when asked what the matter was with her godmother who no longer went out.

—Mrs. *Magui's home needs to be smoked out!*[9] Mrs. Albertina told her husband, Mr. Procópio, a fat and usually absent-minded mixed-race, who, paradoxically, right from day one, had thought his new neighbor to be "a very bizarre person" (an expression he also used when reporting to his wife that he had seen Mrs. Magui in the street wearing a blonde wig).

The most dreadful and well-kept mysteries always hide even more startling ones. The mystery around Mrs. Magui's decision to stay at home because of violence fits this rule. The neighbors could not believe their sight nor their hearing when, at six o'clock, one morning, the

9 A house needs 'smoking out'—*está a precisar de umas fumaças*—when its occupants are experiencing inexplicable illness or misfortune. To resolve the matter, the following steps are taken: burning charcoal is placed in a pan with some olive oil; then some incense is added, as well as lavender, rosemary and fennel; when the concoction begins to smoke, it is carried around the house with the windows and doors shut.

police turned up, arrested Mrs. Magui, covered a blood-spattered body with a blanket, and sealed the apartment,

What the neighbors heard later was what Sandrinha recounted to Mrs. Albertina, her new mother:

—*My godmother used to be a prostitute, just like my late mother. After my mother's death, Mrs. Magui raised me as her own daughter and abandoned her old life to be able to educate me. She left her pimp, moved away, and found herself a job as a housekeeper for a foreign couple. For the first time, I was able to go to school. Gradually, our life started to improve. She began to do a bit of business, bought a second-hand car and we moved into this building. Then her old pimp turned up. I still don't know how he found us! He said he had problems, that he needed to spend a night with us and would be leaving on a trip to Lunda the next day. He ended up staying an entire year living off us! I had to cook for him daily: breakfast, lunch, tea, and dinner... Even snacks! Every night, he would make my godmother wear a blonde wig and sleep with him, threatening to kill her if she refused. My godmother started going mad but she always told me to take care of myself and never to stay alone at home with him... Until that night when everything unraveled! I was sleeping in my bedroom when I felt him getting into my bed. Before I could scream, my godmother appeared and attacked him with a kitchen knife. He didn't even resist, you know!*

Three Endings

The world is subject to the empire of speed. Television reduces reality to thirty minutes of news inserted between commercials every seven minutes. Bill Gates updates his software annually. At every level—state, business, and individual—the decision-making procedures are becoming faster and faster. Investors want to become tycoons overnight. Celebrated authors are writing smaller and smaller novels, perhaps because they are afraid of being considered overly ambitious, while the younger ones crave for fame before they have published a single book. Teenagers communicate through abbreviations on the Internet. The West—which took two hundred years to consolidate its democracies—wants Africans, Latin-Americans, and Asians to democratize and fully privatize their economies, and to allow the IMF and the World Bank to penetrate them in two hundred days without wearing a condom or anything else at all.

Luís Carlos, like many good folks, had never

thought about the issue of speed—which he associated
not only with hurrying but also with anxiety—from this
perspective. Indeed, he even ignored the fact that it could
be viewed as a true dictatorship and produce all these
consequences. Nevertheless, intuitively and perhaps by
premonition, he detested it. And yet, at the very least, this
was contradictory because, since his birth, he seemed to
have been programmed to adapt perfectly to the current
empire of speed, like fish to water as they say.

Luís Carlos had been born prematurely, at just five
months, and had had to complete his development inside
an incubator.

"A baby in a hurry," said uncle Horácio. "He will be
the next Fangio!"

At six months, he began to walk. Aged one, he was
already able to speak his first complete sentence. But he
did not turn into a Fangio or any other Formula One hero.
He wasn't even interested in racing. When Ayrton Senna
was alive, Luís Carlos was happy to hear that he had won
another race, but the Brazilian's "compulsive conqueror"
style, together with his paradoxically androgynous and
frail appearance, left him slightly perturbed.

When he was three, Luís Carlos read a complete
sentence for the first time. At nine, he encountered heaven
and hell all at once when cousin Lourdes, who was already
sixteen, pulled him furtively into her bedroom, nervously
unzipped his flies, and pushed his penis, suddenly and
miraculously erect, into her flaming body. Plunging into

the hot, fluid, and mysterious universe of a woman's flesh for the first time, he experienced an unusual rapture, but it was one that quickly transformed into depressive doubt when cousin Lourdes abruptly pulled away from him, making him spill a strange and unfamiliar liquid all over the sheets. Moments later, passing the living room where uncle Horácio was sitting, he found he had completely recovered. And his uncle said to him, in a voice full of emotion:

—*Champion, go and get a beer for your uncle!*

During his childhood, Luís Carlos steadily overcame the many challenges of growing up and discovered the mysteries of existence, always in short and unpredictable bursts under uncle Horácio's discrete supervision. At eleven, he consciously told his first deliberate and intentional lie, thereby bringing to an irrevocable end, the sweet and naïve—albeit, sometimes cruel—phase of childish fibbing. When he was thirteen, he indulged in theft for the first time: from his father's wallet. He took three banknotes to buy two beers and a package of cigarettes for his uncle Horácio.

What is more extraordinary is that he did all this as if he was irritated, if not regretful. It seems that he was always struggling with an unresolvable internal contradiction; because, though something compelled him to make these early discoveries and to carry out these speedy acts, something else was also always telling him to put on the brakes, to stay put, to grow up in a less obvious

way, to appreciate life more softly and slowly. Then a vast
and bitter melancholy took hold of him. Uncle Horácio,
who was always close by, told him:

—*Don't let yourself get down, kid! Tomorrow is a new day!*
You were born to be a champion!

In contrast to uncle Horácio's predictions, Luís
Carlos did not turn into a Fangio, but at fifteen he got
a job as a driver in a car showroom. His job entailed
testing all the cars — the jeeps, vans, and touring cars—
that were sold by the company before they went on the
market. Whenever he completed any test, he felt nostalgia
for his bicycle which he had secretly used throughout his
childhood, quietly bicycling through the calm and silent
streets in the neighborhood. He used to think, back then,
that when he retired, he would buy himself a brand new
bike to get around at ease and in no hurry.

He married young, to a woman ten years his senior.
By thirty, he was already a grandfather. The day this
happened, he was overcome by unstoppable weeping. He
locked himself in the bathroom for about an hour, and as
he sobbed, he hunted mercilessly for every single white
hair on his head, pulling them out one by one. When
he finally came out, nobody recognized him, except his
new-born grandson, who looked at him and smiled. That
evening, compelled by a bizarre and unbearable impulse,
Luís decided to go to work outside the capital in a sister-
branch of the car company.

In terms of his retirement benefits, working hours
outside the capital were double the normal value. So when

he was forty, legally speaking, Luís Carlos had already worked for thirty-five years. He, therefore, chose to retire so that, as he said to himself, "he could stay alive," a somewhat ambiguous expression that the narrator openly admits is impossible to explain, not only because of the dictatorship of speed that we are all subject to nowadays and which, consequently, causes many narrative gaps and dangerous communication failures, but also because, at the end of the day, nobody cares to explain, as we say, the cards we keep close to our chest.

Naturally, readers can imagine just how excited Luís Carlos was about being able to sleep in for as long as he liked, as well as the fact that he was no longer required to test cars at high speeds, and was able, for the first time, to start doing those things which he had never previously had the time to do, such as learning English and IT. The truth is, however, that during the last few days at the car showroom, where he had always worked, his memory, whimsically, began taking him back to his childhood, which he had barely experienced and which he could hardly remember. "I am going to start my life again, from the moment when I lost it!" he decided.

You may find it odd, but I must tell you that I'm extremely curious to know what this character I have created, this highly contradictory and afflicted one, will do after retirement. He is so persistently broken-hearted by the whirlpool of time that wickedly consumes him, and the quietness and tranquility that he silently seeks. He endures a desperate struggle with what seems to be his destiny, written long ago in the stars by some invisible hand, and which he has tried to define, as his existential project, a necessarily individual mission. I make this confession because I feel that this story about Luís Carlos, a man who hated speed, is coming to an end and yet, he hasn't given me any idea of the fate he wishes for himself.

I can even make another confession: for the life of me, I don't know why I decided to fabricate this story, when the hurried, pragmatic and amoral times in which we live never favor such Hamletian doubts. Wouldn't it have been wiser to have attempted a bestseller, with lots of sex, money, and power? Or a mystical novel set in Palestine? Or a self-help book?

Be that as it may, I would never forgive myself if I left a character of mine half-way through, abandoning him to the arbitrary will of my readers. With all due respect and consideration that I have for the latter, I don't know what you would be able to do with such a character who, I confess, has demanded so much hard work to create, and with whom, despite not being much to my liking, I share a profound sympathy. All readers are perverse and cruel and thus would probably transform my long-suffering creation into a creature that I had never before met. This is not what I would wish for Luís Carlos. Therefore, I am going to give him three chances to end this story well. In contrast to that which was said by a particular Uruguayan author, sometimes life can have happy endings.

The three chances go like this:

Hypothesis one: On his first day of retirement, Luís Carlos took his wife on a world-wide cruise, which they had long dreamed of, but which Luís Carlos' speedy life had not permitted. Therefore, when he decided the date of his retirement, he reserved two spots on a cruise that would depart precisely the next day to return on the eve of his 41st birthday.

The journey lasted approximately one year. It was unforgettable. From the Greek islands, they sailed through the Mediterranean heading towards the Caribbean and then moving south along the coast, arriving in Rio de Janeiro in the middle of a Carnival. They continued down, crossing the Strait of Magellan, then visited the Philippines, went up to Hong Kong, continued to India, advancing towards the East African coastline, visiting Zanzibar and the Island of Mozambique. They turned at the Cape of Good Hope and stopped in on Walvis Bay, they saw Luanda and Lagos from afar, then stopped at Dakar and the Canary Islands and, closing the huge circle, completed their extraordinary maritime journey at the spot from where they had departed, the Greek islands.

Arriving home, Luís Carlos had, in his calm and quiet eyes, a dazzling glow, which his wife saw for the first time in twenty-five years of marriage. The next morning, he was dead. According to his wife, he died peacefully and happily.

Hypothesis two: When he arrived home after his last day's work at the car showroom, Luís Carlos told his wife that, from that moment on, he would have no contact with his old job or anybody connected to it. As such, he forbade her from accepting any correspondence from the company, answering any phone-calls from his old colleagues and, even more importantly, from welcoming them to their home. The very name of the company could not be mentioned in any of their conversations.

His wife thought this strange, since he had never made radical decisions and had always gently accepted the course of his life. But she did not say a word. She thought that her husband had probably grown bitter on his last day at work and that after a night's sleep, he would wake up with a fresh feeling and would forget his decision. Luís Carlos, however, completely surprised her when he woke up:

—*As from today,* Luís said, *I'm not going to leave the house! I'm too tired... I feel I have lived too much.*

Hypothesis three: Luís Carlos completely vanished on the day of his retirement. He did not return home, he did not linger in the bar on the corner where he usually stopped after work, and he did not go spend the night at his son's place as he used to whenever he felt down. Unaware of any secret lover her husband might have had (these terms I've just used are, almost certainly, quite contradictory because, to be honest, nobody manages to keep a lover truly secret), his wife, as soon as she awoke, knew that her husband had not slept at home, and she knew there was no alternative but to report to the police.

Oddly enough, the police had already been informed by Luís Carlos himself. He had sent a letter to the local police station near where he lived—at least, where he had lived until this point—alerting them that in the event his wife told them that he had gone missing, they should not file a complaint because she was mad: he had not disappeared but had simply left home because he was completely tired of her, of the life they had led up until then, and of that neighborhood that was far too quiet for his liking. He had, therefore, simply decided to leave her once and for all. The authorities should not worry themselves about his alleged disappearance, but perhaps— if they would allow him to suggest it—they should worry about his wife's state of mind, considering how disturbed she would be by his decision.

When his wife left the police station with a copy of her husband's letter in her hand, she was pondering the possibility that she was indeed mad, as Luís Carlos had alleged.

Just for the record, the former car-showroom driver had gone to live with uncle Horácio—still a bachelor and a bohemian—and had become his great drinking buddy, or what we call a desbundar[10] friend (this is an Angolan word that can be substituted with the Portuguese expression, *esbórnia*, which means the same thing and which I like because of its, shall we say, glowing power). He went out

---

10 The verb desbundar means to go reveling or to get down. It is
    rooted in the Kimbundu word mbunda.

with him every night and got to know whole new worlds which he had never dreamed of before. He met up with very unusual guys, and fell in love with statuesque mixed-race girls while having to limit himself to sleeping with dreamy, toothless waitresses, whom he promised to marry despite knowing he would never see them again. He also got drunk every day, acquired insurmountable debts, wrestled, and even wanted to kill and to die.

What followed, therefore, is what often happens to many good people: he decided to experience, at a vertiginous and voracious speed, all those things that, for years, he had violently repressed and prohibited himself from doing, like a sinful impossibility deserving of atonement in the most Dantesque inferno. Luís Carlos could have decided to accelerate this self- destructive process, but for him, the matter was something entirely different, even from a moral perspective: he was only making up for the time he had wasted, which, according to what he now thought in this new phase of life, was a fundamental human right to which he was entitled.

I am not going to get tangled up in these sticky and labyrinthine quagmires, especially these days, when different moral fundamentalisms are fighting each other, that would be a foolish display of madness. Therefore, I will merely confirm to my readers that in this final scene about his destiny (at least his literary one), Luís Carlos, after having retired and abandoned his wife, became one of the city's most notorious night owls in living memory. As a simple narrator, this is all I have to say.

Having presented you with three possible scenarios (to which the narrator, perhaps presumptuously, added the necessary details to give each story some credibility) from the thousands that could have been chosen to end the story of Luís Carlos, the man who hated the current predominance of speed, which one should I finally choose so as not to cheat my readers? I don't know. So I ask you, therefore, not to come back to me with this question because I pose it to be post-modern. As such, I am already in a hurry to write my next short story.

Portrait of a Character
in Search of a Writer

Y ou lot need to know my history. Yes, with an H. Do you think it might be of interest to some author? Well, here it is.

I never had a childhood. Or rather, I don't remember one, which amounts to the same thing. I cannot remember anything. Zero. I don't know when I was lifted out of my helpless vegetative state for the first time, nor when I started crawling. I have no clue as to which direction I took with my first steps. I don't know which word was the first to find its way out my mouth.

To dramatize a little bit more, I also have no recollection of the first time I used a potty, brushed my teeth, or ate with a knife and fork. I don't even remember the first time my penis hardened, nor what caused it—something that bothers me to this very day. Of course, I am aware that this elementary information is passed on, second-hand, for everyone, in other words, by a third party. But I haven't even had that.

To cut a long story short, I never had anyone who could tell me what that first period of my life was like, on this planet, on which I happen to live. Likewise, I never had anybody in whose steps I could follow, whose light could be my candle amid the awful gloom that, for me, is human existence; or whose outlook could act as some sort of white flag, flying peacefully but decisively in the center of this constant war, all against all, every day, without exception (please note, regarding the preceding description, the abusive intrusion of poetry, which allegedly and according to a few heartless critics, merely muddles the story).

The earliest memory I have of myself is of someone suspended on two solid legs, but with a completely hollow mind and with a worrying feeling of loneliness and fragility, without knowing what to do nor which path to follow. Instead of being appeased or diluted, this sensation has only increased over time.

Since I have known myself as a person, a kind of paralysis has kept me restrained in the shadowy heart of time. I feel tremendously overloaded by all the individual and collective dramas and tragedies of the world. It is as if my shoulders have had to support the entire weight of the terrestrial globe. I feel permanently harassed by a powerful and complex impulse to do several things simultaneously, but the truth is that I do nothing at all. I don't even have a clearly defined profession. It is true that I have a diploma,

but I don't know what to do with it. I also don't know
how I got it. I do not recall having attended any school,
college or university.

Everybody remembers, for example, their first
primary school teacher. Normally, she's the object of all
sorts of descriptions and impressionistic accounts, nearly
always generous and kind ones, but even when there isn't
much ground for that, they are at least lenient. In my
case, however, my first teacher is a vast black hole. Years
ago, I gave up trying to bring her to mind. Likewise, I
don't remember a single school friend. I don't remember
a single crush, either platonic or consummated, during
childhood, adolescence, or even during my adult life.

Petty sociology—a very useful tool, so it seems, for
contemporary writers—says that teenagers are usually
sexually initiated by their cousins, their domestic workers,
or by the old spinsters who frequently visit their homes.
The truth is that I cannot recall having peeped at any
cousin bathing in the shower or getting dressed in her
bedroom alone, in front of the mirror, oddly fascinated by
the reflection. As far as my memory goes (which means
nowhere), no cousin of mine ever lifted her skirt nor
asked my opinion on the knickers that she was wearing on
that extraordinary day.

Moreover, I can assure you that I cannot recall having
ever tasted (I won't use another, more literal verb because
current times are less and less favorable for freedom,
even useless freedoms, such as the literary type) a single
housemaid. Someone told me that I don't know what I

missed, but please consider such a statement as merely an innocent *fait divers.*

Regarding those possible spinsters, who supposedly visited my home regularly, I must be suffering from some kind of trauma in relation to them, because the truth is that I only remember them in a vague and distorted way in my nightmares. They appear as indistinct, ambiguous, and volatile shadows, never becoming visible. I'm convinced, therefore, that in my past, no sexual adventures took place between myself and any of them.

The fact is, to my knowledge, I've never had a sex life.

I have never masturbated; as such, I don't know, to this day, the sweet agony of feeling one's penis shivering out of control like a moribund bird, before suddenly spilling in successive spasms a thick and slimy jet spraying freely across every surface and object within reach, like a wild and furious waterfall, or an obscenely joyful laugh. May my critics forgive me once again for this second intrusion of poetry, but what do you expect from me—a raw pornographic description? Do me a favor: don't create complications with the moralizing squad.

If in my material on sex, I don't refer to any foreplay, I refer even less to the concluding phase. Believe it or not, I have never known a woman in the sense the Bible itself recommends. To put it another way, I have never plunged into a woman's body. I don't know what it is like to be burned in the fire that, so they say, all women conceal in a secret location within them, nor have I ever gotten lost inside a single one of them. To be blunt: I have never fucked anyone.

Words are indeed symbolic and, once they have been launched into the air, they become not only the author's property but, principally, that of the recipient. So, before you start to speculate and throw suspicion at me, I must add that in all my life, I have never had any homosexual encounters either—not that I remember, anyway. Yes, I know that nowadays, this means that I am going against the mainstream, to some extent, but it is precisely because of this and other things that my history is so incredible.

All that remains to say is that, apparently having not had a past of my own, the future neither thrills nor worries me. I don't make plans nor have any causes, nor do I belong to any organization. I don't even defend my own cause. As a result, I don't quarrel with anyone, not at home, not in the street, not at work. I don't blame my family for my miseries. I don't speak ill of the government or the opposition.

If, for me, the past is a huge black hole, my future is a plain white canvas, upon which it is not possible to fix a projection.

I am an anodyne being.

You do need to know my history right to the end. Do you think a writer will be able to write it down?

Caricature of the Author
as a Young Man

T he Word: just like that, with the first letter
capitalized. HK had been searching for it since he
saw the hallowed poet Pedrito Manungola on television
and decided that he too would become a writer. To tell
the truth, the hallowed poet Manungola wasn't yet thirty
years old, but he was already celebrated. During a poetry
session at the Angolan Writers' Association, he had started
yelling that the greatest Angolan poet was not—as the
propaganda of the regime insisted on telling both the
Angolan population and the international community—
Agostinho Neto. The greatest Angolan poet, including (or
excluding?) the dead ones, was Manungola himself. He
was the only one capable of discovering that primordial
word, the one which was enough on its own and did not
require any other word to be uttered with it (since the
day Manungola heard a provincial commissioner using it

89

while introducing the poet-president and the ministers in his entourage, he had been using it all the time, only regretting that he hadn't had the wit to create it himself) in contrast to what Agostinho Neto and his clique had been thinking throughout their lives.

In those days, the country was going through very complex times. Some people wished to get rid of all the icons, monuments, and symbols from the revolutionary past even though they had not been real revolutionaries themselves—which was why, against the simplest and most straight-forward expectations, they had survived. They had to metamorphose into democrats and liberals, allowing a few demonstrations of rebellion and dissent, especially if such demonstrations were little more than a colorful carnival parade. It is from this neutral and objective perspective that one should, therefore, frame (a verb that evokes older times indeed) or at least explain the invitation to Manungola from state television, following the scandal at the Angolan Writers' Association, asking him to participate in a live program on the hardships faced by young Angolan writers.

That program has not left HK's mind to this day. During the televised interview, Manungola gave a real show, demonstrating his fabulously histrionic qualities. To begin with, he said that political poetry is shit. He said that worrying about the content of literature was a residue of democratic centralism. He said that Jdánov was the son of someone whom he could not mention because he was on television. He said that older writers were too obsessed with colonialism—a topic that did not preoccupy his generation—and that they did not even notice the errors committed by the so-called revolutionaries. He said that, more than being merely discursive, political poems were verbose and cantalutista[11] (itself an unclear adjective created by some Angolans and which will never be possible to translate into Mongolian). He accused the elders of plotting to do everything they could to stop the emergence of new literary values in the country. He said that those of Portuguese descent were the worst because they were always awarded all the literary prizes and were always arguing with young writers who they accused of failing to master the Portuguese language.

"We, the Angolan people, don't need any of this mastering of the Portuguese language," Manungola stressed while staring into the camera and thus, at the viewers, determinedly. "Portuguese is a colonial language. If, in 1975, they packed up all their riches and took them away with them, why didn't they do the same with their language?"

As you can see (and unlike the celebrated author Pedrito Manungola, I am not against the old Portuguese language, also known among us as casputo), this character's discourse is incongruous since, just a moment ago, he was insisting that colonialism did not bother him.

---

11 A neologism invented by a group of Angolan poets who dislike political literature and who use the word to insult poets, especially those linked to the ruling MPLA party, who write political poetry and pamphlets.

So it would seem that this is not the truth after all. Is it not the case, according to his own comments made during his first television interview, that his official name is António José da Cunha, and that he changed it to a more African-sounding one when he started writing? When the interviewer asked him why he was not writing his books in any of the national languages, Manungola got upset and asked the interviewer if he had anything against a young, black Angolan author—one who was living in the slums—writing in the language of Luis Vaz de Camões. A fight was avoided thanks to the director who decided to go to a commercial break.

During that interview (HK still remembers), Manungola, referred to several poets, universally known for their rebelliousness as well as for their innovative spirit and the truly revolutionary (in all aspects) nature of their work. He concluded that, just like these great symbols of creative inspiration and human freedom, he too was craving for justice in his own country. For, until now, and despite having published a book thanks to the sponsorship of the private security company where he worked in public relations, he still owned neither a house nor a car. The interview ended with Manungola standing up and reciting poems in Russian, which he had learned in Kiev, where he had studied the mechanization of agriculture for five years.

It was after watching that interview that HK also decided to become a writer. Given that he was already fortunate enough to have an authentic Angolan name, he wouldn't need to change it as had been the case with António José da Cunha. He became an unconditional admirer of Mallarmé, Rimbaud, Pound, Joyce, Boris Vian, Allan Ginsberg, and Kerouac, despite never having read a single line by any of them—which is hardly important and if it's mentioned here, it's simply for rhetorical reasons. If the celebrated author Manungola, only two years older than he, could, allegedly, write like those sacred monsters of universal literature, what would prevent HK from doing the same?

The Word, however, became a much more painful objective than he had ever imagined possible when he first watched Manungola's interview on state television. First, he tried to do it alone, but his writing made him nauseous such that it never reached the stage where he could show it to anyone. He remained involved in the activities of the Angolan Writers' Association and the Caxinde Tea Association, only to become even more confused than he was before. He tried to buy a book by Boris Vian in one of the bookstores in the city, but the salesman told him that they had nothing by a Mr. Viana. All that remained was for him to speak personally with Manungola. After a series of unsuccessful attempts, he met him at the opening of an exhibition at the Portuguese Cultural Centre. Disgracefully, he failed to get any useful advice out of him at all, because Manungola, like all the post-romantic poets, was completely intoxicated.

"The language, kid." This was the only thing the celebrated author managed to say. "The language is fundamental, kid!"

By the time he got home, HK—who, unlike Manungola, had some principles—had already given up the idea of becoming a writer because, no matter how much he toyed with the idea in his head, he couldn't work out which damned language he was supposed to use. When he did, eventually, make up his mind, he was so relieved that he felt as if he might die.

This is the only aspect of the whole story that I cannot understand.

Maria

The attitude of Maria, who committed suicide and left a single-sentence note—which I won't disclose to avoid having to immediately end this story, which I have not even begun—can be better understood, possibly, if readers know a little bit about her.

By virtue of my position, the onus of introducing her falls on me. I begin by noting that this is precisely one of the most mysterious (or polysemic, if you wish) names used by mankind, one that lends itself to a thousand and one interpretations, connections, and articulations, no matter how conflicting they may sometimes be. Nevertheless, it has quite a simple foundation: Maria is a name without an exclusive, self-centered identity. Anybody, no matter their origin, status, or even their location on our vast planet, can be called Maria. To demonstrate just how in-tune I am with the current hegemonic lexicon, I have no difficulty in telling you that this really is an authentically global name.

For those who are Christian, the merest evocation

(mental, oral, or written) of this name leads us obviously to Jesus's mother, who is considered by everyone to be a saint (whatever that may mean); however, if we look at things from a, let's say, scientific perspective, and with my deepest respect for all Christians, she could rightly be recognized as having had the first womb to be rented out in the history of mankind. Maria was also the name of Magdalene, Jesus's concubine, although this does not authorize me to speculate that the revolutionary Jew suffered, in the end, from the Oedipus complex.

What happened is that, possibly due to its slightly esoteric and cabbalistic origins, the name Maria spread to all regions, nations, and civilizations. If we narrow the focus, we can observe that in any national, regional, or cultural context, the name is proudly used among all social strata and that its bearers (both female and male, as we shall see) pursue very different professions and occupations, dedicating themselves to an almost infinite range of activities. I will leave it up to those readers who are interested in the minute details of work to draw up a possible inventory of such activities.

Maria, on the other hand, is a name that is, as we say, intrinsically flexible, easily adaptable to a wide range of combinations: Maria Helena, Maria de Fátima, Maria do Céu, Maria de Lourdes, Maria Aparecida, Maria dos Anjos, Maria Celeste, Maria das Dores, Maria Haller, Maria Mantena or Maria Isabel are just a few examples. Not to mention, of course, Mariah Carey. All these combinations appear to be obvious, not only by being familiar to those who hear them but, most of all, being socially accepted, even when originally they were freakish or even resulted in unusual agglutinations, such as Anamaria or Maristela. Let's accept that Maria is, indeed, an extraordinary name despite the fact, as fundamentalists across the board would say, it does not possess any features of its own. Or is this the reason for it?

Taking this a bit further, we can also consider Maria to be a rigorously androgynous name or thus perfectly adapted to our current times. As such, it can also be used by men. António Maria, José Maria, Joaquim Maria, Carlos Maria, Roberto Maria are a few examples that can be used to prove this thesis.

The fact is—and I'm now starting, albeit slowly, to reveal what happened to Maria—that she committed suicide because she did not know how to respond to the question. Strictly speaking, she could not avoid the Hamletian doubt that had pursued her right up to her last day. But, if you want to know—as indeed you are entitled to—what doubt we are talking about, don't put too much trust in your cultural repertoire and even less in appearances. How often do we think that we know someone like the back of our hand and then, suddenly, we are taken aback by a disgraceful act by that person, an apparent contradiction with their supposed identity? Please wait, therefore, until the end of this story.

Confining myself purely to our linguistic zone, I must say that, obviously, with this name, Maria could be Portuguese. But how could I, an authentic descendent of Ngola Kiluanji and Bula Matadi, have a Portuguese woman as the lead character in a tale that aspires to be included in Angola's literary historiography and—who knows?—in future anthologies edited by the Papa Doc of Angolan literature, a figure whose name I will not reveal so as not to give him, as we say, free advertising (after all, I'm not here to run errands for anyone).

Maria could equally be Brazilian, without her identity losing any of its credibility. For those who may have forgotten, the independence of Brazil was proclaimed by a Portuguese king on the shores of Ipiranga. Since then the number of ambiguous demonstrations of love between the two countries has multiplied, thus confirming that ambiguity is an unavoidable characteristic not only in the history of mankind but also in this feeling that poets call love. Maria, therefore, is a name that can be found in that country in the same way, according to a widespread stereotype, that we encounter soccer players, samba dancers, and mixed-race women. Or, a wild flower known as *Maria-who-has-no-shame.*

As you know, after the late arrival in Brazil of Matarazzo, Belisário, Tondo, Suarez, Sinclair, Schatschnneider, Ahmed, Lee, Fisher, and many other examples, nowadays the name Maria is mixed freely with all of them, showing not only the etymological and polyphonic lavishness of Brazilian names, but also the remarkable diversity of the country. This information is purely aimed at enriching readers' cultural baggage to help them in any television quiz, but in all honesty, it has nothing to do with the true story of Maria.

Even if it were the case that she was Brazilian, the author would immediately run the risk of being considered a dangerous luso-tropicalist,[12] who should be mercilessly battered—in cold blood, if necessary—and left convulsing to his death. It happens to be the case that I still have children to raise. So, for the peace of mind of those who champion the fundamentalism of black Kimbundu Angolans—many of whom, despite the color of their skin, have Caucasian traces not only in their names but in their family backgrounds too—I shall not be the first to soil our glorious national literature with spurious characters taken directly from the demeaning theories supported by Gilberto Freire.

The truth is that some of them don't miss a single opportunity to regularly visit Rio de Janeiro, where they do not hesitate to mix with some of these characters, gathered as they are, in this particular case, in the Copacabana discos and other local "hellholes." But this, my goodness, is so old that it has nothing to do with postmodernism. Therefore, it does not merit inclusion in Maria's story.

---

12 Luso-tropicalism is a theory associated with Brazilian sociologist, Gilberto Freire, that posited that the Portuguese were particularly good at adapting to life in the tropics and to the culture of the indigenous people they encountered there. Miscegenation and acculturation, argued Freire, resulted in a harmonious multi-racial society throughout the lusophone world. The theory was—and still is—used by defenders of Portuguese colonialism, however it has also been highly criticized.

Just for the record, and despite this name having been transported five hundred years ago by angelic Portuguese sailors, together with beads, mirrors, the rosary, and the cross, not to mention swords and canons, Maria was a genuine Angolan. After so many historical ambiguities and so much confusion, I must confess that I am not quite sure what it means to be a genuine Angolan and so, this is precisely the kind of discussion that I consider to be utterly foolish and useless. I can imagine, therefore, just how much the Byzantines suffered, wasting their time on this matter, simply to discover that Maria, with her name imported directly from that garden by the sea—for which they still nurture a secret and unconfessed love-hate relationship—was a genuine Angolan. And yet, this whole mess is definitely their making.

Had Maria been as wise as I regarding this issue, what happened might never have happened. Thinking it through, however, has been quite handy for me because it has provided me with material for another story and helped me in my attempts to fulfill my commitments to my publisher. The problem with literature is that, often, characters tend to rebel against their creators, refusing to behave in the way that was planned for them and even avoiding the endings that have been reserved for them. I— who, in reality, never had the slightest idea about certain details—advised her to get married to a British engineer and go live in Venezuela. But she wouldn't listen and so, what happened happened.

To avoid you accusing me of being partial, because of

my pre-established notions on some issues, it is better if Maria herself tells you everything:

—*My life is quite simply a contradiction. I am black, at least that is the race on my identity card, although my eyes are green. I am a woman, although I have never had any romantic involvement with a man. I am Angolan, although I don't like funje, semba, or kizomba, nor do I believe that the national football team deserves to compete in the German Cup, and I think that Mozambicans are kind people, despite the fact that many of them die from the frustration that they are not white South Africans of British origin.*

I recall that, as a child, I never played with dolls. The first ones I was given I tore apart, brutally and cruelly, and it made me feel better for some reason that I have ignored to this day. After having destroyed four or five dolls, people stopped offering them to me. Since I liked playing games considered to be masculine, they started calling me "tomboy", but they were soon disappointed when they realized that I liked that. When I finished high school, I decided to graduate in electro-technical engineering, much to my parents' sadness because they had wanted me to become a teacher.

In 1975, when the MPLA declared independence, I was twenty years old and one of the few who had not given up studying or entered politics. What they used to call a "revolution" in those days filled me with a diffused fear, for sure, but one that was also concrete, palpable, and even quite carnal. I completed my graduation and joined an engineering company. The director was a former freedom fighter who had gone to some Eastern European country to do an intensive six-month training course to become an electrician. I didn't like what I saw, particularly the marginalization and even persecution meted out to the oldest employees. However, since I have never been given to making sweeping decisions, I put up with it until the 1990s, when the political and economic spheres opened up.

It was hard for me to understand all the changes, particularly all the misunderstandings that had occurred between us in the past two decades. I could never decide which was worse: the war or the corruption? For a few, war is a thousand times worse because, in addition to its direct consequences, it brings with it a whole set of indirect consequences, such as facilitating and even "justifying" corruption itself. According to history, it seems that this is what always happens in war no matter where it takes place or when. But then, how can it be, the war having finally ended, that corruption shows no sign of slowing down?

Another inexplicable phenomenon that I cannot understand is that since the end of the war, many have begun to nurture extraordinary, if not morbid, anxieties, such as counting how many white, black, and mixed-race ministers there are, and how many white, black, and mixed-race writers, sportsmen and millionaires there are, and how many Bakongo are heading up the health or finance departments, or how many Ovimbundu are judges, priests or bishops. It would be much better instead if these supporters of the ethnic-racial purity of the country could concern themselves with the incapability of the government, and with corruption, hunger, and extreme poverty. (Note from the author: the character is fully responsible for this statement; the author has nothing to do with it.)

It is true (adds Maria) *that I have never given a second thought to living abroad, but it is also true that I am getting more and more tired of living in a place where, were I a more strong-*

minded person, I would have to spend all my time arguing with a bunch of jerks. So I am seriously considering accepting Thomas's wedding proposal. He is a British engineer and has been here serving at a UN agency. I met him a few months ago. He's willing to take me with him to Venezuela, where he is about to be posted, but not before we visit London where I will meet his family.

When I first met him, I fell in love with something he said: "Those who give too much importance to details are deeply unhappy." In all honesty, however, I am not sure I really do love him. As I said earlier, no matter how unusual it may seem, I have never experienced a romantic involvement until now. I have become very worried wondering how I will deal with his family. According to Thomas, his mother would be shocked to see her son with a black woman. He tells me that I will be better off not paying any attention to that, but I am not sure whether I can do this. It seems, also, that regarding the prejudice of human beings, we are all alike. None of us should cast the first stone. The only thing I'm certain of is that I am confused. I am totally at the mercy of my author, who having given me this plastic and ambiguous identity, and this name for that matter, apparently does not seem to know what he is going to do with me. Sometimes, I wish I could die. I cannot go on this way. I must do something.

When Maria's body was found beside a bottle of pills, they discovered, between the fingers of her hand, a note made up of a single sentence. Nobody, however, could read what it said. Not even me.

The Nordic Engineer

Before coming to Luanda, where he'd been sent by the oil company for which he had worked for over thirty years, Jan Andresen started reading up on the new country he was soon to explore (literally). A Nordic engineer, who had raised two children and was happily married to Ruth Andresen, he was a lover of words and the simple pleasures in life. In addition to Portuguese classes and several long and extremely boring lectures about Angola led by some of his predecessors, he watched several videos and requested for a few books by various Angolan authors—which caused some problems with the company's secretary in Luanda who, despite being an Angolan herself, swore that there were no writers in the country.

The Nordic engineer read the likes of Luandino, Arnaldo Santos, Jacinto de Lemos, and other authors who, with resolute stoicism, have demonstrated that Luanda exists and that, at least in terms of literary raw material, is much more succulent than Jorge Amado's Salvador, or even Macondo and all those other fantastic cities recreated by García Marquez. However, the reading that excited his curiosity the most, due to the grotesque exoticism of the setting, was a novel by an Angolan minister about the Roque Santeiro market. This novel is considered a masterpiece of Angolan literature by some and by others— who were perhaps jealous of this ministerial intrusion in the literary field—as mere bullshit.

At any rate, Jan Andreson, after his readings, began to believe that Luanda was a city like any other. On his arrival, he asked to be taken to the famous Roque Santeiro market ("The largest informal market in Africa!" according to the typical Angolan show-offs) to try some grilled goat meat. Coincidentally or not, after eating the grilled goat meat, Jan Andresen developed an appalling stomach bug that left him prostrate for a week, shitting as if he had been condemned to death.

"But what city is this?" was Jan Andresen's question when he eventually awoke.

Jan Andresen's unfortunate experience came to the attention of the locals and deeply divided the political class. For the opposition, it revealed, once again, not only the government's vast inabilities but most of all, its profound lack of sensitivity towards the people's problems, because for some time now, the goat-grillers of Roque Santeiro— and others—had been demanding better working conditions to help reduce people's hunger, or, if not the hunger itself, the appetites of all the foreigners, at least those who demonstrated exemplary multiculturalism, who loved tasting national dishes and refused to live off imported and canned products.

In turn, those who—due to one of the many mysteries of mankind—supported the government, reacted to the opposition's attacks by asking several simple but highly insidious questions:

"And his driver? Where did he come from? Why did he take the Nordic engineer to Roque Santeiro without any security? Why did he not take the piece of goat out of the man's mouth? Why didn't he give him an enema?"

The minister of home affairs himself went on national television to say that all those who dared question the government's commitment to improving the city's hygiene were followers of Savimbi.[13] (At the time that these facts were being conjured up, being a follower of Savimbi was much worse than being a son of a bitch). The minister added that he would warmly welcome anyone who, in good faith, would contribute to the reconstruction and development of the country.

One of the private newspapers, known for its iconoclastic bent, took the opportunity to start a fierce campaign against Islamic fundamentalism, accusing all goat grillers of being worshippers of Allah. This strategy increased sales of the paper for a few weeks, but when the numbers began to fall again, it suggested, with the subtlety

---

13 Angolan politician and rebel military leader of the National Union for the Total Independence of Angola.

of an elephant, that the Nordic engineer's diarrhea had nothing to do with grilled goat nor with the flies that populate the city as if it were their own home, but that it was, in fact, the so-called "disease of the century."

Today, when Jan Andresen recalls all these, he smiles condescendingly but also with sincere happiness and comfort. His life took a turn that no one, apart from the author (pass the immodesty, but if I don´t do my own commercial, who else?), could have imagined. In one fell swoop, he'd left the oil company which had seen him turn grey, and bought a farm in Viana, where he grows porcelain roses that he exports to the Netherlands, and where, at least once a month, he enjoys grilling goat for his friends.

Death Is Always Punctual

Dr. Carlos had been clear and decisive:
—*Private Kiteculo has priority!*

Nobody knew for sure which day the plane would come with food and ammunition, or if it would come at all. The situation on the ground was ugly. The unit was almost surrounded by the rebels and, in the air, there were constant raids by the South African air force in an attempt to prevent government planes from landing and replenishing the troops—who, for more than a month, had been fighting to keep control of a strategic position—as well as airlifting out the most seriously injured.

Private Kiteculo was among them.

The day before, he had lost most of his jawbone during a South African bomb blast, when shrapnel hit him mainly in the face, but also in the chest and arms. The episode occurred during a reconnaissance mission led by General Ambrósio, in whose group Private Kiteculo belonged, to an area five hours' walk from the command bunker and field hospital. When the South African air force came into sight, General Ambrósio instructed everybody to hide, but Private Kiteculo was among those who didn't have enough time. Be that as it may, he was lucky it was only his jawbone.

The return to camp was made at night, more or less three hours after Private Kiteculo's jawbone had been hit. Adding the five-hour walk to the command base, Private Kiteculo had been losing blood for eight hours. Fortunately, the improvised dressing made by his comrades shortly after he was hit, had been applied so well that he survived. At first dawn, when he entered the field hospital, he was visibly weak but oddly, cheerful.

Dr. Carlos was woken up in a rush to attend to Private Kiteculo, who had been the most seriously injured during the reconnaissance mission. General Ambrósio himself had gone to wake him, this being a delicate task, as he knew. Every evening, Dr. Carlos would not go to sleep without polishing off an entire bottle of *Famous Grouse* whisky, because—the doctor claimed—he had suffered from insomnia since childhood. On this particular night, General Ambrósio, contradicting everything in the military manuals, had to shoot in the air to wake up Dr. Carlos.

The latter, to be fair, was a true professional. When he arrived at the field hospital, located two tents away from the one where he slept, he was already wide awake, with all his senses fully functional. After a quick examination of

Private Kiteculo's jawbone, he shouted:

—*We're going to operate on this guy!*

The truth was that the conditions to carry out such a procedure were not available, however, everyone agreed that it was necessary to operate on Private Kiteculo.

The anesthetic wore off before the end of the operation, which lasted more than four hours, however, Private Kiteculo's jawbone was now back in the right position. He would require some aftercare, which could only be carried out in Luanda.

The supply plane was scheduled to arrive at noon the next day, and Dr. Carlos' order was clear and decisive:

—*Private Kiteculo has priority! If he is not taken to Luanda immediately, he will die!*

The next day, the plane had not arrived by five o'clock in the afternoon. This meant that it would not be coming.

Two days passed and the plane did not arrive. The military situation had gotten even worse and, while they were on the ground, they were battered more systematically and more often by the rebels. In the sky, all they could see were South African aircraft. The military command in front sent a column with reinforcements, but it met great resistance along the way. General Mau-Mau, the head of operations, was beginning to get worried.

Private Kiteculo continued to withstand his injuries.

Dr. Carlos visited him every day. Three days after the surgery he had felt compelled to make, he asked himself how such a successful operation had been possible.

Indeed, Private Kiteculo's jawbone had been put back into its original position, the patient had no fever and, although the stitches made it difficult, he had also started talking again. What amazed Dr. Carlos most of all was that he had never carried out maxillofacial surgery before. Was this thanks to *Famous Grouse*? The thought made him smile, although it was a rather bitter and painful smile (or a sympathetic one? He couldn't explain…).

Whenever Dr. Carlos went to visit him, Private Kiteculo told him the following:

—Doctor, I actually saw the South African planes but when General Ambrósio told us, "Get down! Get down," I felt scared because I was already on the floor with my face in pieces!… But it seems that my time had not yet come…

—You were very lucky, Kiteculo! Dr. Carlos would respond, *but you must go to Luanda…*

The aircraft's delay was beginning to worry Dr. Carlos. There were not adequate conditions in the field for Private Kiteculo's recovery. In addition to the almost inevitable possibility of him contracting a post-operative infection, which under such circumstances would prove fatal, the rebels were getting closer and closer and could take military control of their position at any moment. Given their well-known and very bloody practices, they would spare nothing, nor anyone.

Two days later, the troops heard the sound of a plane approaching the base. But they could not see it because it was flying very high to avoid the rebel's anti-aircraft tactics while trying to find a place to land. On this particular day, such an opportunity did not emerge.

—*Private Kiteculo cannot take much more of this,* Dr. Carlos told General Mau-Mau. *He must go soon to Luanda!*

The latter limited himself to the following response:

—*That's war, doctor. That's war!*

That night, Dr. Carlos couldn't sleep because the bottles of *Famous Grouse* sent from Luanda by his girlfriend were already empty and he hadn't been able to find "something similar," as he referred to the bottle of *massango* brandy that he usually managed to order from the nearest village.

When dawn began to break, he had some kind of "revelation" about Private Kiteculo which rather distressed him.

—*Fuck! I fixed his jaw and I know nothing about him!*

Private Kiteculo didn't have a lot to say. He was a young peasant from Huambo, who'd ended up going to war like all the other youngsters, especially the peasants, not only from Huambo but from every Angolan province. His parents were also from Huambo, as were his grandparents and his grandparents' grandparents. Until he had gone to war, the world was as large as his village, where he lived with his parents and his four grandparents, both paternal and maternal.

He did six months of army training in Malanje, then he passed through Luanda and was sent to the North, where he remained for over a year. Afterward, he was integrated into General Mau- Mau's brigade and sent on this operation into the remotest part of the country. The war had, at least, helped him discover the size of Angola. It also enabled him become acquainted with all sorts of Angolans, whom he never knew existed. He himself helped populate Angola with one such Angolan, because in Uíge he left behind a son he'd had with a mixed-race girl from Cabinda. When he left Uíge, she wanted to leave with him but not even he knew where the war would take him next.

—*And you, doctor, are you from Cuba?*

—*A Cuban? Bastard prick! I am as Angolan as you are!*

Dr. Carlos was a white Angolan, whose family originated in Italy and Portugal but had been in Angola for three generations. The family had remained in the country after independence, except for a younger sister, who married a young black civil engineer, whose father was said to have been a member of the Portuguese secret police during colonialism. After completing his graduation in medicine in Luanda, Dr. Carlos had joined the armed forces. This was the third time that he had been involved in a large military operation.

Like all human beings in this sort of situation, Dr. Carlos and Private Kiteculo engaged in conversation about what they would do once the war was over. Every day, while they were waiting for the right conditions for the supply aircraft to land, they confided in each other about their post-war plans, something that everybody longed for perhaps even more than the defeat of the enemy. They were both aware that the post-war period was even less likely than the plane's arrival, but even so, they could dream.

Private Kiteculo's dreams were limited, like those of any peasant. He longed only to go back to his village, to embrace his parents and grandparents once more, and to farm his land again. But, on the third day's conversation with Dr. Carlos, he let something out:

—*Before that, I must go to Uíge to fetch my wife and my son!*

Dr. Carlos thought about his girlfriend, who was in Luanda and who, as often as possible, would send him bottles of *Famous Grouse*. And yet, the excitement that used to accompany such thoughts quickly turned into profound sadness, as if, right at that moment, his soul had been hit by thousands of thin and unexplained pieces of shrapnel. What would become of their relationship once the war was over? Would their love survive the post-war period? He decided to take the conversation in a different direction.

—*Don't you want to go to Luanda?* he asked.

—*But, Doctor, haven't you already said that I'm now going to hospital, there in Luanda? Or isn't the plane coming?* responded Private Kiteculo.

Shit, the plane! Yes, the plane would come, the plane had to come. If the plane does not come, this guy won't make it. The jawbone is in the correct place, but he is in a state of general weakness. Here, food is running short and the column bringing reinforcements cannot get through. What else can I do for him, damn it, besides what I have already done? I had never done such surgery before, for fuck's sake, and I still don't know how I managed to put his jaw back… It must have been a miracle!… It's true that this guy also helped himself because he's as strong as a bull. But, without food, he won't be able to withstand it much longer… And anyway, he needs another blood transfusion, and our stock is finished… This plane cannot be delayed much longer!

—*Of course, the plane will be coming, Kiteculo!* said Dr. Carlos. *Don't worry… Right, enough chit-chat! You need to rest… Sleep tight, soldier!*

As he was walking towards his tent, to try to get some sleep himself, Dr. Carlos thought, fleetingly, if it wouldn't be better for him, after the war, to get a piece of land somewhere in this area and become a farmer. Naturally, a smile spread across his face.

On the seventh day after the surgery, the supply plane was able to land, at last. General Mau-Mau welcomed the pilot, Muxi, in quite a strange way:

—*Where have you been, you son of a bitch? Boozing, or what? For six days, I have been waiting for you!*

The General then laughed and hugged the pilot so hard he almost crushed his chest.

Weapons, ammunition, and provisions brought by pilot Muxi were unloaded in less than an hour and transported to the tents that were used as warehouses and arms depots. The arrival of that "order," as the troops called it, rapidly changed the mood in the base, as if a good spirit had passed over it. General Mau-Mau told the cook:

—*Prepare some funje and chorizo for everybody. And make*

it quick because the pilot has to take the plane back again.

Dr. Carlos was already with his crate of *Famous Grouse*, sent by his girlfriend in Luanda. He took a bottle and offered it to General Mau-Mau.

—*General! Can I get the wounded ready?* he asked.

—*Only the worst ones, doctor! We are in a mess and I need every man here...*

Anyone who can hold a weapon must stay, because early tomorrow morning, we will start our counter-offensive.

—*Well, Private Kiteculo is the only one seriously injured. He's the guy with the jawbone...* explained Dr. Carlos.

—*Yes, I know. That one can go!* said General Mau-Mau. *I just hope that in Luanda they get him a proper mouth! The way he is right now, I can't see any girl wanting to kiss him,* he added with a laugh.

Dr. Carlos called two nurses and rushed to the tent where the field hospital was in place.

—*Comrade, today you will be going to Luanda!* he said to Private Kiteculo. *You will return from there with a brand-new mouth!*

A strange sense of melancholy took hold. It lasted no longer than a second, but the silence that, all of a sudden, developed among them, just before the nurses put Private Kiteculo onto the stretcher, worried Dr. Carlos. He couldn't quite understand the question the patient had asked him:

—*Doctor, if something happens to me in Luanda, how will you inform my parents in Huambo?*

—*Eh? What? No, no, you will not be stopping in Huambo.*

The plane will fly straight to Luanda... You must get to the hospital very soon, otherwise, you will die!

Once the stretcher carrying Private Kiteculo was on board, pilot Muxi said:

—*Welcome on board, comrade! Please fasten your seat belt as we will be spiraling out of here and we don't want any surprises! I want to reach Luanda as quickly as possible because I've got a party later...*

The aircraft took off, and in the air, it reared up its nose as much as it could and, from a certain height, started flying in spirals, one after another, higher and higher. The afternoon was silent and crystal clear. The sun had lost its afternoon glow, but it was still bright. No roar from any hostile aircraft could be heard and the rebels' artillery was mute; just a few birds, indifferent to the momentary hidden presence of the war, insisted on chirping into the air. Everything seemed so calm and perfect that General Mau-Mau told all of his men, apart from the sentries, to take a rest. The next day, they would be breaking the siege that had held them paralyzed for a whole month.

Dr. Carlos was the only one who saw it all: the silent and treacherous flight of the missile, the fuselage breaking in two, the aircraft crashing into the nearby jungle, and exploding in flames. All of a sudden, the afternoon was jolted and covered in blood.

Canivete Has Gone White

To Sembène Ousmane

I t's true, yes sir, I had already promised that I was never going to speak any more balderdash, slang or swear words, many use them, but, yet, however, notwithstanding, although many do not like reading them, my wish then was to look into their eyes and call them hypocrites, frauds, fucking church wardens, but thinking it over perhaps there is a difference, words when spoken are carried on the wind, but when written down on paper, just so, black on white, that's it, as commanded by law, they remain forever, able even to lead a man into misery, and that is why, in the past, whites took advantage of blacks, who didn't know how to read or write, making them sign certain strange papers, *It's just for the record, Mr. Kiteculo, you know how it is, one of us may die and, afterwards, no one knows what was agreed between us*, they would say, the truth is that what was written on those papers would only bring us misfortune, Canivete himself told me many stories full of such misfortune, back then he was still black like me, I am not sure if I should say this but Canivete also liked to use strong words, those really foolish ones, we were working back then as assistants to Mr. Antero, a white truck driver who travelled from Benguela to Moxico, who (well, now that I'm started, I may as well tell it all) also used to talk a lot of nonsense, such that, once in a while, especially when we were caught in the middle of some nightmare, a flat tire in the street, or some really time-consuming unloading, or an argument with some customer, our conversation would be like a symphony of nonsense, mockery and profanities, a strange word that, I don't know why, insisted on inserting itself into this part of the text, then, in order not to lose the way, I can go on to say that, in fact, the three of us really enjoyed opening our mouths really nice and wide and pouring out as many profanities as we liked, against everything and everyone, starting with our good selves, but when the words had vanished on the wind, we would have a beer and continue on our way, Mr. Antero driving, and me and Canivete in the back, of course, catching the sun, the rain and the wind, because in those days that's how it was, these were the rules and full stop, if I knew how to use irony I would say, for example, that back then these protocols took precedence, the truth is I didn't pay that much attention to it, my relative position within the physical structure of the truck, struck me as, so we say, a mere detail, to be honest I could not have cared less about traveling inside the cabin with Mr. Antero due to another detail that I can now reveal at will, that is his extraordinary, radical and absolutely unavoidable foot odor, but Canivete, unlike me, was always complaining about this fact, he did not like to travel in the back nor did he like to catch the sun, the rain or the wind, but most of all he did not like knowing that Mr. Antero travelled in the cabin all by himself, well-protected and sheltered, even from the profanities (look at that nice, polite word once more) that were being shouted out behind him, *Who do these settlers think they are? One day this is going to have to end,* I can only give these two examples, unfortunately, I cannot be as true to Canivete's words because I don't want you to call me ill-bred, I can't stand that label anymore, also I have my children to raise, though for a long time now I have not known their whereabouts, they are also lost like me, amid the vortex of events that have shaken our land, Canivete seemed like a fortune-teller, in those days he would say *Angola must change,* today, when I remember those words, I don't know if I should laugh or cry, Angola has changed, yes sir, but here I am sitting next to the most luxurious restaurant in the city, protected by the shade of the night, ragged, dirty and most of all starving, waiting for the left-overs from dinner, without anywhere to go after the last customer has left, thinking about Canivete's words, *Those settlers think that we are just dogs or what,* and I am going to speak my truth, with a profound nostalgia for the back of Mr. Antero's truck, of course I do not know if I should have written those preceding words like that, black on white, but, look, they are written, as I said before, for me to travel in the back or not was always a simple detail, while Canivete was complaining all the time about the sun, the rain and the wind, saying as much nonsense about Mr. Antero as he possibly could, and when I mentioned to him the matter of cheesy feet, he replied, *The guy has smelly feet, but he also has money,* it was mainly in these moments that he told me stories of the strange papers that would only lead to misfortune when suddenly the white guys would appear in the villages, saying *This land is ours!*, and completely surround them, using guards they would start to exploit them in a way that was completely different from that which the villagers had learned from their ancestors, the chiefs could do nothing, the spirits would not listen to the prayers of the men, who, ever weaker and more bewildered, were pushed further and further away, some of them were even forced to depart for remote and unknown regions where they learned new skills and engaged in new occupations, at least this was what Canivete used to say, *I have never been an assistant truck driver!*, I didn't really understand these words very well, partly because I had never been an assistant truck driver, it's true that I had never been a farmer either, for I was born in the city and the only other occupation I remember having had was as an errand boy in a shop, but when Canivete added, *And I shall not be an assistant to a truck driver forever!*, the solemn tone and drama that he impressed upon the sentence filled me with curiosity, but at the same time I couldn't help a certain, albeit badly defined, fear from piercing my heart, I continued racking my brains, this guy too, this guy too, he knows nothing, like me, if he won't be an assistant to a white man, he will do what then, this question does not have a question-mark for one supremely simple reason, I was only asking myself, I didn't have the courage to put these words (or better, this thought) to Canivete face to face, because of the way he spoke the sentence, *I won't be an assistant to a truck driver forever!*, I was afraid, yes, I was afraid of this sentence, but I was even more afraid, truly petrified, of the expression on his face when he uttered it, Canivete would grit his teeth, frown, look deeply into my eyes and then he would say the whole sentence, *I am the son of a traditional chief, I have never been an assistant to a truck driver in my life and I shall not be one forever!*, and when he finished, he would stare at Mr. Antero, who wasn't aware of anything at all because he was by himself in the cabin, protected from all threats, both physical and symbolic, to tell the truth, I was more afraid of that than Mr. Antero should have been, at least for believing in Canivete, *The guy is alone in the cabin because he's afraid, he knows that our time will come!*, he said, so what could my argument be, when based only on a small and somehow ridiculous detail, against such an absolute and categorical statement, *Foot odor, so what!*, responded Carnivete when, unwisely, I insisted on this detail, *You're afraid of whites, or what? Historically they are condemned...*, at that I had no other alternative but to shut my mouth, the truth is that Canivete knew nothing, like me, he had had no education at all, but sometimes he seemed to have

indisputable wisdom, and that scared me, I was okay with
the life I had, I enjoyed traveling in the back of Mr.
Antero's truck, I already knew all the places between
Benguela and Moxico yet still I always had some surprise
on every trip, Mr. Antero was not such a bad white man,
his biggest problem was that he used a lot of swear words,
but keep calm, I am not going to reproduce any of them
here, I have already promised that I shall speak no more
drivel, profanities or, as some call them, obscenities, and
will write them even less, black on white, without any
respect for my morally correct readers, for all these reasons
(or intuitions, how can I know?) I considered Canivete's
claims to be a little exaggerated, but, yet, however,
nevertheless, there weren't big disagreements to have
with him, the truth is that I enjoyed continuing to hear
the stories that he told me about misfortune, adversity and
harm caused by the whites since they had arrived in our
beloved land, us two lying down on top of all the goods,
watching the changing landscape or looking at the sky,
enjoying the clouds during the day or the stars at night,
while Mr. Antero's truck rolled quietly along the roads,
without the boss even considering the profanities that his
assistant Canivete was saying from the rear, to him and to
his whole race, my keeping silent, listening, at the same
time sad for all the sufferings of the Angolans and delighted
by Canivete's stories, admiring each word, the wisdom
and courage that was so clearly in all of them, but always
with that unknown fear that pierced my heart when
certain words were released from his mouth, the grit of

his teeth, the red shadow in his eyes, the way he would suddenly be quiet and stare at the back of the neck of Mr. Antero, who didn't feel a thing, as if for him, Canivete, words were no longer enough, ah!, but I shall reveal to you all my truth, when those words weren't there anymore, I missed them, very much indeed, and I felt lost, the landscape that I had come to know so well, after so many trips made over so many years, gradually lost its ability to surprise me, every day I saw the same clouds and the same stars, the same places, the same people, all the same, however the oddest thing to happen to me during those times was that I started looking at Mr. Antero in a different light, the poor guy may have robbed and exploited many Angolans, let's be honest, but he never caused me any harm, however, despite that, I started looking at him with disapproval, answering him slapdash, one day he even asked me, *What the hell is up with you, boy,* I did not respond because the fact was that I too did not know what the matter was with me, the fact is that suddenly I became very angry with Mr. Antero, for me, he was to blame for Canivete's disappearance, when I asked him he said no, he liked him very much, how could he be to blame for his disappearance, he had always respected Angolans, without any discrimination whatsoever, the fact was that he was merely a truck driver just trying to earn some money through his own work, this was, in brief, how Mr. Antero responded to me, so, if it is impossible to know the truth, whether in life whether in literature, all that remains are facts and these can be summarized likewise, Canivete disappeared one day without warning, in the middle of a journey between the former Silva Porto, Kuito today, and the former city of Luso, now Luena, Mr. Antero had stopped at a gas station just after the border between Bié and Moxico, it was six o'clock in the evening, therefore he told us that we were going to sleep there for the night, in order to depart very early the next morning for Luso, I remember it well, as if it were yesterday, he was particularly friendly towards Canivete, *Take care not to run off to join the terrorists...*, he said to him, laughing, what is strange is that Canivete was also in a good mood and offered him an unexpected reply, *Only if the boss comes with me!...*, we laughed the three of us, Mr. Antero gave us some money to buy a bottle of wine to accompany our funje, then he went for dinner with the owner of the gas station, an old friend of his, who always invited him to spend the night in his guest room while we slept, as always, in the back of the truck, that night, after eating our funje and emptying the bottle of wine, Canivete did not tell me any stories because he was very tired and wanted to go to sleep straight away, early the next morning, when I woke up, he had already disappeared, nobody knew where he'd gone, nobody had heard a sound, Mr. Antero started arguing with everybody, swearing in every direction, in every language that he could, Portuguese, his own mother-tongue, but also Umbundu and Luvale, the languages that he had learned to speak with Angolans, *Dreadful terrorist! Dreadful terrorist!*, this is the only printable expression in all the swearing used freely by Mr. Antero, since that day I am completely alone in the world, without Canivete's stories, without his words that terrified me, but pointed to a different future, *Angola will change!* he used to say, yes, Angola has changed, soon after Canivete's disappearance, April 25 happened, the Portuguese army signed up for peace with the three liberation movements, a transitional government was created in Luanda, composed of the former terrorists as Mr. Antero used to call them, independence was marked for November 11, 1975, in the cities the war re-started between the three liberation movements, the Portuguese began to flee, loaded with boxes, taking everything they could by plane, by car, by boat, even by trawler, the FNLA brought the Zairians, the white South Africans entered, with their armored vehicles vomiting fire out of their mouths and their yellow helicopters, Cubans came to help fight the South Africans and the Zairians, Agostinho Neto managed to declare independence on November 11, and FAPLA and the Cubans drove out the Zairians and the South Africans, the MPLA adopted Marxism-Leninism as the ideology of the regime towards the end of 1976, in 1977 there was an attempted coup d'état in Luanda, the president of the United States of America, Ronald Reagan, decided, in 1980, to transform UNITA into his principal instrument for overthrowing the MPLA government, in the 1980s Angola was practically divided into two states, 1989 saw the mutual departure from Angola of both the Cuban and South African forces, in 1990 the MPLA renounced the one-party system, abandoned schematic socialism and installed wild capitalism, in 1991 the Angolan government signed the Bicesse Peace Accords with UNITA, in 1992 the country's first general elections took place, won by the MPLA and by president José Eduardo, to the despair of the former Portuguese president Mário Soares and his son João Soares, who can't help grumbling even at the thought of it, UNITA rejected the electoral results and restarted the war, in 1994 another peace agreement was signed between the government and UNITA, the Lusaka Protocol, but the war continued until the February 2, 2002, when the rebel leader Jonas Savimbi was killed in combat in green-and-white-striped knickers, when he was getting ready to listen to the radio commentary of the Sporting-Guimarães football match as part of the Portuguese championship, which led to the signing of the Memorandum of Understanding by the government army and UNITA troops on April 4 the same year, definitively stamping peace on the country, until now, at least, there has been no more shooting, the real truth is that I didn't know all the facts mentioned above, they are the author's unique responsibility, I limit myself to living in the flesh through the unbelievable changes endured by Angola during the last few decades, I lost myself in the whirlwind of events that I saw and not just that, drifting around the country I was in the war, on both sides, randomly producing several children who I do not know, leaving them even more haphazardly, I fled, I was an artisanal diamond digger, then I ended up in a refugee camp in Namibia, now I am here in Luanda, I have no home, I have no family, I have absolutely no one, I live on the streets, I wander through the city, my latest spot is outside this restaurant, here I come every night at around eleven o'clock, waiting for the leftovers from dinner, as well as a few coins from some full stomach, like this one, for instance, who is arriving now in his huge jeep, I mean the model seems to be a *Hummer*, as this kid Tony is in the process of telling me, these young good-for-nothings know everything about cars and motorbikes and not just that, the driver of the jeep opens the door for the big-bellied being, who climbs out of the car with style, hanging on to a dark, skinny thing with blonde hair extensions that almost reach her buttocks and hide her own smattering of curly hair, a dress with a split to the thigh, shoes with heels almost half a meter high and stiletto toes, the sort that kill cockroaches, big belly held her close to him, he gave her a pat on her pert ass, perhaps to help her relax, as they walked swiftly towards the door of the restaurant, when the light shines on their faces, I feel like jumping up and shouting, Canivete, Canivete, I hesitate, it really is him, isn't it, I have not seen him since he disappeared in the gas station on our way to Luso more than thirty years ago, but the truth is that I have not forgotten him, not for a single day, every day, along the paths in which I lost myself, I hoped to find him, yes, I know I mentioned this before but the truth is never too much, when he disappeared I was left abandoned in the world, desperately missing the stories that he used to tell me, his words full of contradictions, uplifting and threatening, how could I ever forget Canivete, it is really him, he is different, he looks white, where has he been all these years, what has happened to him, what have they done to him to make him so different, I don't know, but the author, once more, is obliged to know, come on man, tell us readers what happened to Canivete, well, nothing extraordinary, half a page will do, when Canivete disappeared on the road to Luso, at the gas station where Mr. Antero always stopped to spend the night, he joined up with a group of MPLA guerrillas with whom he had maintained contact for some time already, he was with this group for just two days and then he was sent to a base located on the border with Zambia, where he arrived just in time to be incorporated into a group of young people who were going to study in the Soviet Union, he stayed for ten years in that country, studied at the Patrice Lumumba University, considered by the reactionary forces (do they still exist?) of the world, I do not know why (I have already said that irony is not my strong point), to be a "university for blacks", he returned to Angola in the 1980s with the title of commander, although he had never fired a gun in the guerrilla war, he was appointed director of a diamond company, in the early 1990s he gave an interview in which he swore that he had never been a Marxist-Leninist, he became provincial governor for a few years but was discharged under suspicion of having sold fuel to the rebels, now he is one of the best-known genuinely Angolan entrepreneurs, with businesses in every sector, import- export, commerce, industry and services, livestock farming, fisheries, consulting services, publicity and marketing, and is particularly appreciated by the press, both public and private, and for his support to culture and arts, because he is one of the major sponsors of the famous Brazilian singer Roberta Miranda during her regular visits to Angola, as you see, I had my reasons not to trust Canivete when he used to say that he would not be an assistant to a truck driver forever, I felt like swearing really badly, but I promised I would not do that again, Angolan literature, in the current phase of reconciliation that we are, fortunately, living through, must not only be politically correct, but also morally, this is my last thought before getting up and hugging Canivete, I shout *Canivete! Canivete!*, the guy really does seem to be white but I am certain that he will recognize me, now, yes, my life is going to change too, the man has turned into a big belly, therefore he can help me change my life, to leave this wretchedness into which I sank after he had disappeared, I shout again, *Canivete! Canivete!*, the guy gives some order or other that I do not see, but I become scared when two private security guards, a policeman, and the driver of the white guy, who looks like Canivete, grab me and start beating and punching me, preventing me from embracing him like in the good old days when he was a black like me, and the truth is that I got so confused in my mind that I even forgot the promise I had made to my dearest readers, I really couldn't help it, I opened my mouth, which had been shut for such a long time, and I said, black on white, clearly pronouncing every syllable, *Shit! Cock! Fuck you! Go back to the bitch who bore you, you white motherfucker,* I hope you can excuse my bad manners, but the truth, however, is that in this land of ours that is Angola very strange things are occurring, completely improbable things, such that people are left with their mouths wide open, even people who fought in the struggle have forgotten the reasons why they did so, now they are acting like the colonialists did in times gone by, or even worse, now Canivete, for example, has become a white man too, he who was as black as I, these extraordinary things that we never agreed upon, and with all this sadness that we have in our hearts, all we can do is loudly mock and loudly swear, as I have just done.

Aunt Holy

*A*unt Holy was a saintly woman. Indeed, only a
saint could put up with uncle Féfé, her husband.
An inveterate womanizer, lazy, a drunk, a bully—he was
a true well of flaws. Nevertheless, Aunt Holy used to say:

—*My Féfé is the husband I asked for in my prayers!*

Nobody could understand it. A certain poet said
once that "the heart has reasons that reason itself does
not know." Since none of us, however, knew of that
particular poem, we could only assume that Aunt Holy
was suffering from some mental illness. We didn't jump
to the conclusion that she was mad, crazy, nuts, or had lost
her mind, full stop because she didn't seem like that at all.
As Ruca, who was studying to become a doctor, would say,
she didn't have any symptoms.

Aunt Holy was who common sense would call a
good soul. Tranquil and quiet, when she had something
to say she would say it, as we say, in a half-voice, using
a tender and sweet tone, which, although very pleasant,

133

sometimes made it hard to understand what she said. On those occasions, she would repeat the phrase, without demonstrating any irritation or showing any impatience until her interlocutors had understood her, without margin for error or misunderstanding.

Some gossipmongers said Aunt Holy wouldn't speak for fear of her husband. Every time we went to their home, for some reason—a lunch, a party or simply to drop in—Uncle Féfé monopolized the entire conversation and prevented practically anyone else from talking. He did it in such a loud voice that, if he didn't intimidate everyone, he tired us all out in such a way that nobody tried to get a word in. Aunt Holy, for her part, didn't even attempt to open her mouth. On the contrary, she was always ready to satisfy the many requests that Uncle Féfé made—to fill up his plate with more funje, or serve him another glass of wine, or clean *"with hot water and lemon!"* the stain of palm oil from his shirt—practically screaming and without even looking at her.

Given the, let's call it, noisy regime to which she was eternally subjected, it was predicted that Aunt Holy would try to compensate the marital dictatorship—a classification that was ours—created and maintained by Uncle Féfé, by making the most of any of the latter's absences from home, or, better still, using the absences to, let's say, catch up on her talking. If, instead of "catch up on her talking" you would rather use a more formal expression, in line with the current global political discourse, you could substitute it with "to exercise her legitimate, sacred, and unwavering right to freedom of expression." But avoid saying, for example, "to exercise her throat," because of the ambiguous and disparate interpretations that this sentence may encourage.

The truth is, however, that Aunt Holy simply ignored all of these alternatives, that is to say, when Uncle Féfé was not at home (which, I cannot repeat enough, occurred a lot), she would remain systematically and permanently quiet, opening her mouth only to say something essential, in such a way that her communication with others could be classified as merely factual. Everyone who lived there in that house—and even us, who only visited—knew Aunt Holy's character.

With her neighbors or, more accurately and with no preconceptions about gender, with her female neighbors, things were exactly the same. Aunt Holy could have taken advantage of Uncle Féfé's long absences and spent her days chit-chatting and gossiping with them, but she couldn't care less about this age-old practice of humanity, which some may call "hearsay" and others, more respectfully, as "tittle-tattle."

What is more extraordinary is that, during the thirty years or more that she lived in that neighborhood, nobody ever heard of any argument between Aunt Holy and any of her male or female neighbors. If such a thing had ever happened, I am sure that Aunt Holy would have enjoyed our full understanding because psychology itself grants humans the unwavering right to transfer to others their traumas, complexes and, most of all, their anger. So, according to what we understood, Aunt Holy's mind should have been filled with traumas, complexes, and anger because of the kind of life Uncle Féfé afforded her, a verbal form which may (I have just been made aware of) within the context of this account, be substituted more accurately with "imposed on her."

However, and as I have already said, Aunt Holy was a saint. Because of this, she never argued with any neighbor, male or female, even though some of them, as you might expect, were not the sort of flowers you wanted to smell. Similarly, when a neighbor complained to her about her husband's alleged or true villainy, she would only say,

—*My Féfé truly is the husband I asked for in my prayers!*

As I have already said, Aunt Holy's blind devotion towards her husband confused us, sometimes even really irritating us, not only because of Uncle's Féfé's bad nature in every sense but also because of the small amount of time he devoted to her.

According to the information we gathered, he had two other women, this being the reason why we never saw him at Aunt Holy's place more than two or three times a week at most. One of those days was compulsory, Saturday, when Aunt Holy would prepare a huge lunch at home, although she herself would eat very little. She just loved seeing everybody there in her house, welcoming us all with just a few small words, but always with her sweet and kindly manner.

We were, therefore, all asking ourselves how Aunt Holy, such a gentle and refined lady, could endure such a situation. Could it be down to fear of Uncle Féfé? Was she under a spell? Would she not leave him because of some outrageous secret that could not be revealed? Tina, the intellectual in our group, developed a most interesting theory to explain it all.

—*There is no mystery, whatsoever,* she said. *Just think a bit! Aunt Holy hardly speaks, she eats very little and won't leave Uncle Féfé, nor does she creep about with any other man, despite the fact he spends most of his time with other women. She is, certainly, one of these frugal beings, who need little to satisfy her, be it in terms of food, affection, sex, whatever!... As I read in an article a few days ago, there are people like this...*

It seemed that Aunt Holy felt good about her life. This proves the thesis of an Indian philosopher I read somewhere, according to whom the form and measure of the happiness of each one of us are rigorously personal and insurmountable. I must lend this philosopher's book to Tina...

Aunt Holy was in her early fifties when Uncle Féfé died. To be more accurate, he was killed by the lover of a skinny bosomless bird (albeit with a provocative ass) from the neighborhood, who Aunt Holy's husband was desperate to taste. It seems that the chick's lover, a lieutenant colonel, highly crazed because of all the wars in which he had fought, caught him *in flagrante delicto*, in nature's clothes, not having any other option therefore than to throw him out of the current story, without honor or glory. The narrator is grateful because he would like to offer Aunt Holy another and more interesting destiny, after the life she has experienced at Uncle Féfé's side. I hope she will give me a hand, meaning that I hope she will, at the very least, do her part.

When Uncle Féfé passed away, Aunt Holy didn't cry much. Knowing her, as we do, this should not be interpreted as a belated and discrete demonstration of her discontent regarding the way she had been treated by the deceased when still in possession of his vital signs, but merely as a natural corollary of her frugal nature, as Tina would say. Indeed, none of us expected Aunt Holy to cause any fuss about his death. The lack of any genuinely outstanding occurrences does not mean that the mentioning of that detail by the narrator is, therefore, a simple editor's note, without any concrete or effective significance, as is demanded by the good ethics of the journalism of the spectacle that currently prevails in this world in which we live.

What we were hoping for, at least, was that Aunt Holy, after completing the normal period of mourning for a widow, would let her life follow a new path—that she might start to speak more, find herself a job, and most of all, a new husband. After all, she still had everything in the right place and, surely, could still give a man a good time, a rather rude expression—I acknowledge that—but one I cannot help using. As you know, words are what they are: we have the illusion that we can manipulate them, put them into perspective, and use them strictly according to our discursive strategies, so often arduously thought through, but then they break free and bend in different directions, reaching new and totally unexpected targets. Could this be why—it strikes me now—Aunt Holy did not enjoy speaking very much?

I don't know. The only thing I know is that she persisted in nurturing her virtual muteness even after Uncle Féfé's death, which undermines the theory that her silence was due to her fear of her scoundrel of a husband. Likewise, she maintained the same pattern of behavior—sweet, soft, and kind—towards her neighbors. She even persevered, every Saturday, in having the usual lunches—which, formerly, had been demanded by Uncle Féfé—saying that they were some kind of homage to the deceased, which exasperated us profoundly, although, of course, we would not miss a single one. As we noticed soon after the first lunch post-Uncle Féfé, she had also retained the habit of eating frugally. In sum, despite her liberation from Uncle Féfé's dictatorship, Aunt Holy had not changed.

In fact, she seemed so well-adapted to her status, as we say, of eternal widowhood, that when we visited her, and after listening to us for hours with her usual tranquility, she would unexpectedly break the silence to utter a phrase which we knew really well:

—*My Féfé really was the husband I asked for in my prayers!*

Listening to this, we all became caught up once again in those old doubts about Aunt Holy's health of mind. Ruca, however, continued to insist that she had no symptoms. As far as Tina was concerned, she had given up trying to understand Aunt Holy "scientifically."

—It's a spell, she said. *The old bastard must have had powers we didn't know about!*

—Poor Aunt Holy!

I could not accept it. To be honest, I had never liked Uncle Féfé. Everything about him irritated me: his air of arrogance, his authoritarian attitude, his excessively loud voice and, most of all, the way he treated Aunt Holy. Nobody knew, but I had secretly elected Uncle Féfé to be my archenemy. Fortunately, there is a saying that "those who tell the truth deserve no punishment." I may, therefore, admit that I was always waiting for some misfortune to come his way. When he died, I felt relieved and satisfied.

Then I began to observe Aunt Holy more carefully. She was already over fifty, but she was in better shape than many women in their thirties. Because she had never had children, she still had a good figure, starting with her voluminous breasts about which—I confess—I used to dream. Her beautifully shaped mouth that she always painted red, also won my attention. But what surprised me most of all—forgive my candor—were her buttocks, perfectly round and moderately protruding, which, despite being protected by the discrete and modest clothes she always wore even after Uncle Féfé's passing, attracted me like a magnet. Whenever Aunt Holy walked down the street, swaying with perfection, my eyes would follow the movement of that divine ass of hers right up until she passed around the corner or went into some place somewhere, losing me in my contemptible reverie.

Because of all this, the strange postmortem fidelity that Aunt Holy maintained in relation to that brute, Uncle Féfé, upset me immensely. To avoid tormenting myself even further, I began to reduce the number of visits I made to her house until I wasn't dropping in on Saturdays for the memorial lunches to celebrate the departed. How could I pay tribute to my very own rival, especially when my secret and outrageous desire to taste his widow would not leave my mind? Indeed, it was increasing with every day that passed.

One day, Aunt Holy met me in the street and asked:

—*So, dear boy, why don't you drop by anymore? Don't tell me that you were only fond of Uncle Féfé?*

On this day, I resolved to act like a man. As I have always heard, a real man does not entertain doubt. That is for literature.

—*Aunt Holy!* I began.

—*Aha…?*

—*Aunt Holy, wouldn't you like to marry again?*

—*Oh, boy! You think I'm wandering about looking for a husband, or what? I do not need that, see?* She hesitated for a bit, before finishing:

—*Fortunately, Uncle Féfé sexually satisfied me right up until the last of my days!*

She made this astonishing revelation without raising her voice, in that low tone that was always so characteristic of her.

Aunt Holy was indeed a saint.

The Scoundrel

or obvious reasons and, I hope, understandable ones, I will have to tell the current story in the third person. Furthermore, I will not give any name to its main character, thereby discouraging the critics, at least, from trying to identify any personal relationship between the choice that necessarily would have been made and the biography of the author. "He" is how the character will be economically referred to in the lines that follow.

Given that we are, therefore, dealing with a living creature that—I can assure you—is completely separate from both the author and the narrator, I can speak of him openly and without the slightest leniency, or, put another way, without pussyfooting about. Consequently, I shall begin by saying, as the title of the story already suggests, that he was an absolute scoundrel, completely shameless, with all the attributes that define a being—let's put it that way whilst drawing attention to the possible linguistic paradox—worthy of this classification.

It occurs to me now that I could simply have said that he was a downright rogue, an over-used and perhaps abused expression in terms of so-called common sense. I have avoided it, however, for the simple reason that it might convey some kind of sympathy with the latter (the rogue or the common sense? That's for readers to choose...) To use it would be the same as writing that the scoundrel, whose story I intend to tell, was an exemplary husband and loving father, Ultimately, my neutrality as an author risks being shamefully exposed.

He was a scoundrel, no more, no less. But, in his favor, I must add (hoping that this won't be seen as a sign of complacency on my part) that, unlike many, he was not a multifaceted scoundrel, but, yes, a specialized one. I'll try to explain it myself. It so happens that although scoundrels can be classified in several categories—from the political to the entrepreneurial ones, the financial or social ones, the intellectual, artistic, professional, and even sexual ones, among others—the general rule, with each of them, is that there are signs, indicators, elements and manifestations that usually overlap with several of the other categories. Political and entrepreneurial scoundrels, for example, are nearly always sexual scoundrels too; intellectual scoundrels can be often mistaken for political and social ones; and so on and so forth. It is fair to say that specialization has not yet occurred in this type of activity—of scoundrelism—which, curiously enough, is as old as humanity itself.

As generally happens in all areas of human existence,

it is also the case with this particular activity that there are a few exceptions to the rule. So, among other rare species, some political scoundrels are sexually inactive, and certain intellectual scoundrels are, or, at least, allegedly are, apolitical. While there are no conclusive studies on the subject—does literature need them?—most of these exceptions are found within the category of sexual scoundrels. Apparently, being a sexual scoundrel does not require any political, entrepreneurial, or professional crookedness, although the same cannot be said regarding the necessity, as we say, to associate sexual crookedness with intellectual crookedness, at least in rhetorical terms. After all, and as we all know, so-called "cajoling", "chitchat" and "puff" are the tools of the trade for a sexual scoundrel, at least in the early stages.

For some reason, those in the latter group are the only truly professional crooks. This can be explained by the fact that they have to concentrate so much on their very specific activity, dedicating themselves systematically, forever stimulating their imagination to constantly generate new ideas, developing ever more creative strategies, and adopting ever more risky tactics, such that they do not have the spare time, intelligence, innovative capacity or energy for other endeavors. Sexual scoundrels, in the precise and rigorous sense of the term, are the only full-time scoundrels. Furthermore, and as a matter of principle, they hate being mistaken for other kinds of scoundrels. *"Together, but not mixed up!"* they say. Therefore, whenever they can, they commit perfidious acts of sexual crookedness against other scoundrels, for instance, by seducing (with all the ensuing consequences) their lovers and even their wives.

He was one of these authentic sexual scoundrels. To characterize him with a bit more precision and accuracy, I might add that he was, so to speak, an old-fashioned sexual scoundrel, not to say, as I'm sure some readers would prefer, a conservative one. The fact is that he was homocentric in the strictest sense of the word, which, today, many dislike.

The most outrageous thing of all, I tell you, is that he was not in the slightest bit ashamed to acknowledge this. Forgetting, regrettably, the current requirement to maintain a politically correct attitude at all times and to avoid reproducing the sclerotic, male-chauvinist discourse introduced by mankind's patriarchal system, when he was criticized for his crooked sexual conduct, he would say, foolishly and arrogantly:

—*It is true: I like women! What's wrong with that?*

At some point, he even decided to raise provocation to the clouds, whenever he was introduced to someone, by adding an appendage to his Christian name:

—*Heterosexual!*

Beyond this, as was the case with sexual scoundrels across the board, nothing could be used against him.

I am not going to reveal what his profession was, for this would lead readers to endlessly speculate about his identity. But I must say, from a professional perspective, he was truly exemplary. Competent, dedicated, and possessing a proven spirit of enterprise, he had carved out an impeccable career all the way to the top. One detail that shows that he was never a professional scoundrel is this: he was never promoted at someone else's expense. Empathetic, he never tried to overthrow a colleague: on the contrary, he was always ready to offer his support to anyone in need, without ever asking for anything in return.

I will also not reveal his political preference, if indeed he had one at all. That would be a tremendous mistake on my part, because we live in a society that is highly politicized, to the point that this is a phenomenon verging on perversion. Just to give two examples, writers are either deified or detested in line with the political position expressed in their work, as well as those who read them, critique them and "back" them; offenders are rejected, or not, depending on the political colors. I will not, therefore, betray my own character to those bandits. One thing I can guarantee: he was not a political scoundrel either.

He was never a social scoundrel either. Proof of this is that he was never married. I am not saying all married men are scoundrels. All I am trying to explain is that one cannot be a married, sexual scoundrel without also being, of necessity, a social scoundrel too.

Indeed, historical experience shows us that it is objectively impossible for someone to be a married, sexual scoundrel without having a double or triple personality (there are even some who would take this up to infinity), and without being sly or a systematical liar. Believe me: to be married and, at the same time, be a sexual scoundrel is hard work. But with him, this was not the case: what we are dealing with is a truly full-time sexual scoundrel. As the saying goes, if you've got it, flaunt it.

—*In this life, I've already had more than a thousand babes!* he would say when, for some reason or other, he felt the need to boast about his performance.

But readers, don't think that just because he was neither a professional, political, or social scoundrel that this lessens in any way what—I repeat—he really is: a hard-hearted sexual scoundrel. As I have already explained, I do not have any kind of link or even vague relationship whatsoever with the character of this story, nor do I nurture towards him any kind of sympathy or even hidden complicity, and I can assure you, once again, that I shall not be lenient with him.

Like all sexual scoundrels, he had an abominable flaw: he loved boasting about his bad behavior, as if it was, so to speak, a socially significant achievement. Thus, he spent a lot of time flattering himself about this or that woman he had seduced, especially when referring to two kinds of women in particular: those fantastic ones who stop traffic, who can bring a dead man back to life, and who can transform an atheist into a staunch mystic—to use some of the crude expressions he liked to use—as well as those who looked as if butter wouldn't melt in their mouths, werewolves dressed in sheep's clothing, or sly slappers, as he labeled the so-called difficult ones. As is well-known, these two types of women are often grouped as the same,

who we, mere mortals, consider to be utterly out of reach.
For him, it was not so.

—*They all love it!* he said. *All you have to do is find their
weak point!*

He liked sharing with us his know-how, as he called
his seduction techniques. These techniques are as old
as humanity. Times change, naturally, but the concepts
and strategies endure. After all, promises, gifts, dinner
invitations, and parties are all part of the sexual scoundrel's
arsenal—just as much as (no pun intended) a man is a man.
I will not, therefore, enter into any details. But I cannot
go without sharing with you, my readers, the following
curiosity: dinner invitations were one of his favorite
strategies. His justification was even more peculiar:

—*Guys! If she won't go to bed, at least enjoy a good meal!*

He was such a rascal that, as well as boasting about
the women he seduced and the methods he used, he did
not refrain from sharing with us the most intimate details
of his multiple love affairs. Some of the details were truly
disgusting and only increased my revulsion for him.
Nevertheless, I am compelled to share a few with you,
if only to give this story some credibility. Otherwise, you
may accuse me of pre-judging the character without any
material evidence whatsoever, or, at least, without a real
clue.

As such, and as he confirmed on several occasions,
the backseat of his car was one of his favorite places for
making love (he would say, "*for getting it on with a girl*"). But
he didn't limit himself to simply inviting a girl to join him,

then taking her somewhere and immediately afterward, annihilating her (another one of his phrases) inside his car. He enjoyed driving around the city in the early hours, after leaving some joint, with a girlfriend sitting in the back, whom he would have asked to undress completely. Slowly, he would drive like this for ten to fifteen minutes, taking the wheel in his left hand and, with the right one, caressing the naked woman sitting in the back seat. This would give him a hell of a hard-on (I am still faithfully reproducing his words). So much so that, when he pulled over and joined her in the back, an authentic firework display would erupt. He never had any trouble with the police.

Another time, he told us, he invited a professor for dinner. She was six or seven years older than he was. During the meal, he had an idea:

—*Dearest, wouldn't you like me to touch you up a little? Go to the toilet and remove your knickers! I have a surprise for you…*

And so she went. It followed, throughout the rest of the meal, that he spent his time caressing her clitoris with his big toe, while they were eating, drinking champagne and exchanging foxy looks with one another. Since they were sitting at the most discrete table in the restaurant and, moreover, the tablecloth was covering it completely, almost to the floor, they could be as intimate as they wished. What happened after pudding does not need spelling out.

These are two more or less publishable examples of

the unscrupulous behavior in which he specialized. When I think about them, I feel a deep unease, if not to say anger, resentment, and even hatred towards him. Is this just old and prosaic jealousy? I will leave this to you, readers.

A few days ago, having not seen him for a long time, I bumped into him by chance in the street. He looked the same, not only physically, but also psychologically misogynous, as ever. The postmodern androgynous mutation, so to speak, didn't seem to have reached him. Yet, somehow, he looked more mature. Refined?

—*I've already told you that in my lifetime, I've had more than a thousand women. But you need to know that I've also been turned down more than a thousand times!*

At some point in the conversation. He added:

—*The secret is to keep trying! Now, for instance, my target is a little white Angolan, one of those with a fabulous pair of buttocks. They have started appearing in town, though God knows where from!*

I was losing my bearings. This scoundrel should be severely punished, at least literarily. What is there to stop me from doing that?

The Baptism

For quite a long time, the priest had Godofredo on the tip of his tongue because none of Godofredo's children had been baptized. It made a terrible example of the inhabitants of the town; so much so that Father António Maria, when he took up his new post and learned that Godofredo's children were still part of Satan's entourage, immediately decided to launch a crusade against the heretic Godofredo. Thus it was that Godofredo came to be named every single day at the six o'clock mass and on the Sunday mass at eight o'clock in the morning.

As most people know, priests are specialists in parables, which often means that sometimes even their simplest citations tend to be quite oblique and diffuse. This was true with Father António Maria, who, while conducting mass, began to speak about…names, and how every single name, before being anointed, is not a name, indeed is nothing at all, perhaps only a sound, completely without meaning and, most importantly, without future. And how the descendant of anyone who can only whistle but never appoint, is not a true descendant, but a pack of the devil's tiny emissaries sent to terrorize the herd of that lost place. Fortunately, God has sent him (him being Father António Maria) on an uplifting mission to return Beelzebub to the flames of hell, where he should never have left in the first place.

Godofredo, of course, did not understand a word of the priest's tirade. He was known to be quite good-natured. In fact, this supposed heretic, a mixed-race man many considered "a peaceful soul" who "wouldn´t hurt a fly," was fat and calm. Moreover—miracle of miracles—he went to mass, daily, never missed any, even the ones where his name was mentioned.

Father António Maria considered Godofredo's good-natured mien and frequent mass attendance as the height of impudence and pretense—a strategy well-known to Sirius, the dog star. Therefore, though for a while he pretended that he was referring to no one in particular, the priest began to share his parables while staring at Godofredo, his eyes never deviating so much as a millimeter. At first, this disturbed Godofredo, who returned the priest's gaze to see if it was simply that the priest did not recognize him, or whether the priest had some particular preferences that the devil himself was spinning. But over time, especially during the eight o'clock morning mass, Godofredo—who, like many good-natured, fat, calm men, liked to booze a bit, especially at the weekends—couldn't resist taking a good nap even as the priest stared at him while speaking about anonymous herds and other crazy things he must have learned in the seminary.

But on one occasion, the priest decided to give up on his parables, and address most clearly, the case of one Mr. Godofredo Ramos da Silva, whose children had still not been baptized, a failing, the priest insisted, was of deep concern not only to the Christian community in the town and surrounding areas, but most of all, it was a concern to the Lord Himself.

When Godofredo heard his name, he was startled awake from his nap. To this day, no one knows why he abandoned mass with such a decisive and resolute air—in contrast to his trademarked phlegmatic character—while, at the same time, looking so serene and happy. All who witnessed his departure that day were left completely intrigued.

Godofredo never again went to church.

Father António Maria took the episode so personally that, ever since, he has been on the verge of a nervous breakdown. His tongue completely lost its wits. His sermons against Godofredo, people said, became explosive. If it were today, we would have argued that "the mouth of the priest is a police station", an expression which means that Father António Maria could end up sending someone to jail.

Anyway, as happens with all aspects of life, too much of anything becomes a bore. Therefore, although this was a small town in the Angolan interior, where, naturally, there wasn't a lot going on, Father António Maria's crusade against Godofredo ceased to be a novelty and wore itself out. The priest was forced to suspend his sermons against this man who refused to baptize his children. While in the cosmos, the earth continued to revolve around the sun, the townsfolk continued to love themselves and hate themselves, to bury their dead and to make new children, who would inevitably repeat the habits of their parents and grandparents.

So Father António Maria experienced an authentic revelation when he was invited by an envoy of Godofredo's to christen the latter's children. The priest arrived at Godofredo's house where he lived with his three wives— one black, the other mixed-race, and the third an albino. There, in the middle of the house, in an enormous courtyard, stood all the children waiting to be baptized: all thirty-two of them, in all shapes, sizes, and colors, and all dressed in white as recommended for such occasions by the venerable Catholic church. Everything was ready for the party that would inevitably follow.

Father António Maria, who recently arrived in Africa from Beira, and who was at peace with himself and God, could not stop smiling when Godofredo, as good-hearted as ever, explained what had prevented him from baptizing his children for such a long time.

"My problem was how to find thirty-two different names, father! Do you know how I resolved it? I went to some people well-known to me (six or seven of them, I can't remember now) and I told them that if they would each choose five or six of my children and become their godparents, they can name them as they please!"

Angola Is Wherever
I Plant My Field

It was the war that brought me here, I did not chose this place, I was not looking for anything, I was doing very well in my village, the war came, my memory refuses to remember when, all I know is that this memory has not let go of me, it has glued itself to my skin, speaks through my mouth, looks through my eyes, shakes my legs, and explodes in my ears whenever I hear a bang, no matter how meaningless, a thunderstorm, the exhaust pipe from an engine, a door thrown open to its miserable fate by the wind, all of a sudden we were terrified, we saw the men who had entered our village, running in all directions, shouting, shooting at any moving thing, people, goats, chickens, the whole village was consumed by flames, at first I thought *these men are mad, they are shooting at random, there are no soldiers here, what is going on in their minds*, then I understood, kill, kill, just kill, we were trying to run away, what else were we going to do, just flee, each to his own, men, women, elderly, children, all running for our lives, escaping the village by any means, escaping death, not once turning our heads, there was no time, we would see later who got away, the men coming after us did not appear to be men, or perhaps this is what men are like, always were, always will be, and we are the ones who insist on believing otherwise, endeavoring to invent something else, but we don't get it, men were running after us, angrily firing shots, their eyes were transformed, and they were speaking a strange language, the language of war, however necessary, at times, at least according to some, must be decreed incomprehensible forever and always, the day we understand it will be the day we accept it, the men pursuing us were slobbering like hyenas, I didn't manage to get a good look, they really wanted to kill us, why, I still don't know, but it is not even worth asking, I saw people falling around me, but even now I don't ask why they died, I will never ask this question, indeed I swear, it is not worth asking a question for which an answer simply does not exist, indeed when someone dies for no reason what is the answer to that question, besides, if there is no answer whatsoever, why ask the question, what is certain is that the day that the war arrived in the village where I used to live, all I could think of was fleeing, like everybody else for that matter, but each person fled according to their survival instincts, the men behind us got closer and closer, the breath of death drawing dangerously close to the nape of our necks, people we had known since we were born fell beside us, hit by gunfire, the day was getting ever darker, through the intense flames of war, time had almost stopped, hanging by a thread, the end of the world was coming, but even so we did not desist from fleeing, we kept on running, each one his own way, trying desperately to find shelter, behind trees, beneath the ruins of houses, in the bush, in the river, the men always giving chase, trying to kill us, but what evil had we done to them, none, so why do they wish to kill us, this was the only question that crossed our minds in that moment, no sooner had it been formulated, mentally, of course, than our own minds would ask it, automatically, as if somehow it had been wound up, but this question was like the other one, it also had no answer, even worse, the answer was so frightening that it was not worth hearing, I was running towards the river, all the while posing this useless question inside my head, when some other men arrived, they began to advance towards the first group, who had to recoil, they were no longer aiming at us, we didn't look, we carried on fleeing as far away as we could, the second group of men and the first group of men began fighting each other, I asked once more, at least back then I liked asking questions a lot, why are these men fighting, the village is completely destroyed, in truth it no longer exists, it's over, the majority of the people have died, others, a few, fled and had more luck, if you can call it luck, this fate that the Creator reserved for me, oh Nzambi,[14] look at my misery, my village is no more, the war has swept it off the map, my wife, my children, where are they, it seems that they were killed, now I am here, in the middle of the bush, not knowing where to run, I left the men back there exterminating each other, I don't want to look, I don't want to go back again, these were the thoughts I had in those moments, when I was trying to escape the war, despite everything, yes, I was lucky, really lucky they didn't manage to kill me, I fled, plunged into the river and swam until I reached a forest, where I walked alone for three days, only eating fruits, until I came across a patrol, first they took me to their barracks, then they brought me to this camp where I am now, in Luanda, well, this is not really Luanda, but it is near enough, I wish I can go to Luanda, but I won't go because I hear there is too much confusion there, here I am OK, I won't leave here again, yesterday they came to ask me if I wanted to go back to my home, how am I to respond, this is another question without an answer, when I came here I found few people, but everyone had fled the war like me, I confess a truth, I did not know that Angola was such a big country, oh, people from everywhere, new places, new names, new faces, but in fact I feel like I have known them for ages, we quickly became friends, they told me about villages I did not know of, some had different names, they were not villages anymore, but, yes, towns, cities, provinces, I knew

14   Nzambi Mpungu is God for the Bakongo people.

nothing of this, but they explained it to me, now I know, after all, there was war everywhere, in the villages, in the towns, in the cities, in the provinces, not a single corner escaped the war, these people came from everywhere, at the beginning, when I arrived, they were just a few, but over time their numbers increased, as the war extended reaching places that no one thought it could reach, the people, whenever they arrived in the camp, they always had plenty of stories to tell, much misfortune, great suffering, they needed to pour out their souls, I understood, but I always refused to tell my story, when I arrived here, I took a decision, not to get imprisoned by my past like a bird in birdlime, I must open my eyes wide to see beyond, into the future, most people don't know this but the future depends on the way we look on the past, you may ask, what about the present, I only have one answer, the present is worth nothing, the present is a will-o'-the-wisp, the present is a bridge, the present is a path that we cross to reach the river, it may be a dangerous journey littered with obstacles, zombies, and chinganjes[15] lost in the night, but it is still a path we must cross, if it is dangerous we must cross it even quicker, those who spend too much time in the present, perhaps trying to decode the signs, to appreciate the detail in the landscape, rummaging through the supposedly final motives of people's decisions, forgetting that they are always provisional, they continue,

---

15 *Chinganjes* are masks with special powers that are used in rituals to call upon the spirits and forces of nature.

in truth, to be locked in the past, fearing its return,
therefore they do not advance, they never manage to reach
the future, when I arrived in this camp I said that my
future is here, if someone had heard me they would have
said this man is a mad man, does a displaced man have a
future, it seems that he does not fully understand where
they have put him, this camp has nothing, only half a
dozen tents, people have to sleep on mats, in the open,
hospital, never, school, never, even toilets, you can forget
it, they defecate in the open, the government has brought
them here and abandoned them, they did not die in the
war but they will die here, the more intelligent ones have
already gone to Luanda, to add to the roboteiros, the
kinguilas, the zungueiras[16], the whores and thieves,
perhaps they will make it in that holy mess, but the
majority will wear away and rot here, I said no, my future
is really here, when I said this camp had nothing, it is true,
nobody knew when the war was going to end, that's also
true, but I saw beyond this, I looked directly into the eyes
of the future, I chose a piece of land and planted cassava
and sweet potato, I got tired of the yellow maize flour
from the WFP[17], so I went to a nearby farm and asked for
some seeds for tomato, lettuce and onion, I planted them
next to the cassava and the sweet potato, the other people

---

16 In Angola's informal economy, *roboteiros* work as porters,
transporting goods in their handcarts; *kinguilas* are male and
female money-traders, usually exchanging US dollars and
Angolan kwanza; *zungueiras* are peddlers who sell all sorts of goods
from containers carried on their heads.
17 United Nations World Food Program

who had fled the war like me, mocked me, they told me I
was crazy, I waited, when the land propagated the tomatoes,
the lettuce and the onion that I had planted, like the
miracle of Jesus Christ when he multiplied the fish, I
started selling them on the street, with the first earnings I
bought wood, with the second I bought strips of corrugated
iron, with the third I bought nuts, bolts and other
materials, I made myself a house, with a toilet and
everything, the others were amazed, they stopped laughing
and started thinking, laughing and thinking are not
incompatible, of course, but only when the laughter has a
concrete and fundamental cause, gratuitous laughter is
alienated laughter, as they used to say in the old days, to
laugh is a serious matter, so, my friends, this is why I
laughed, satisfied with the world when I woke up one day
and saw people cutting the grass all around the camp in
order to be able to start planting too, in a few months the
camp was transformed, at first three new houses appeared,
then seven more, then fifteen, then suddenly the war was
over and we held a party, then one day an official from the
government turned up, accompanied by two white
women from an NGO, along with a group of foreign
journalists, to report on the situation of the war's displaced
people, so that they could ask for another United Nations
donation, I noticed that the two white women looked a bit
annoyed, perhaps because their funding was going to be
reduced, the war was over, we had started to look after
ourselves long before, perhaps they would have to return

to their own lands, leaving behind Miami Beach,[18] Mussulo,[19] some Angolan who had secretly consoled them, to help them forget the mosquitoes, who knows, the government man took advantage of the situation to talk at random, *What you can see here, gentlemen, is an example of the authority's new strategy to teach people how to fish instead of giving them fish, as the Chinese say, the Angolan people, as well as being generous, are highly enterprising, the experience in this camp can be replicated across the country in no time at all, our strategic goal is to reduce our dependency on donors, but obviously we still need some support, there still remains much to be done, for us it is rather frustrating to feel that the international community is shunning its responsibilities, after all, Angolans did not make war on their own, you were the ones who pushed us into it, I say this on behalf of myself,* the governmental official continued, *Angola is a country with fabulous resources, that's true, but they are yet to be fully exploited, anyway, what kind of country has the ability to rebuild itself alone, without international support, after experiencing the kind of war as the one that ravaged ours, not even Germany, ah, you want a contemporary example, gentleman, well will Afghanistan do,* the governmental official went on for ages, time was passing, before they left without hearing from us once again, we said that *today we do not want any filming, we want to be able to speak freely, why do you all like coming here so much and stealing our images, showing them to the world, when the world has never listened to us directly, the*

---

18 A beach bar in Luanda

19 A tiny but idyllic island just off the Luanda coast, where wealthy Angolans and expatriates spend their weekends.

*photographs that you have been taking also rob us of our dignity
and our soul, if you do not want to help us it would be better if you
forgot us completely, to help, you have to listen to us, how can you
know what people think, what people need, what people want, if
you only take the photographs that your bosses tell you to take, if
you only think about the value of a project, if you only listen to your
own speeches,* I was addressing them all indeed, without
exception, the government official, the NGO activists, the
foreign journalists, but to this day I do not know if they
understood, the problem is that everyone refuses to see
what we want to show them, they close their ears to what
we tell them, even though our words are simple, as simple
as are our wishes, we just want to live, to forget the war, to
build something, to educate our children, even here in
this camp we need support to build houses, with a
backyard, with a toilet, we want to farm the surrounding
land and sell our products, we want a school, a hospital,
we want a television so that we may watch what is going
on in Luanda, and also the world, they say that beyond
Luanda there is a huge world, they noted down everything,
the government official nodded, the two white women
asked to be filmed with us and we allowed them, they left,
we carried on with our life in the camp, each day there
was a new field, two or three new houses, over time a
market was set up near the camp, from Luanda came rice,
sugar, salt, canned food and other products, and into
Luanda we sent tomatoes, lettuces, onions, fruit, cassava,
sweet potatoes, even goats and chickens, then the first
taxis started appearing, the young, mainly, began going to

Luanda, I also went once, I won't say if I liked it or not, but I did not stay, for I am sure that my future is in this camp far from my village but which welcomed me as if my mother had been born here, my memory has even forgotten which day the war came to my village, my life has changed completely since I arrived here, I met a woman who had also fled the war, she came from a village that I do not know, because I cannot speak her language, instead, we speak Portuguese, the colonizer's language from whom we freed ourselves, we are very fond of each other, we live together, we already have two kids, the school is taking its time to appear, the hospital too, but I know that they will build them, if they do not, we will, the present is worth nothing, I have said it already, what matters is the future, but the future is much more than a promise, an illusion, a fallacy, the future is only the future if we make it, it is not from the sky that the future will come, first, the future is born in our minds, then it is built by our own hands, there is no need to search too far for the future, the future is everywhere, but it is not something you ask for, we must search for it with care, then we will build it without ever losing heart, the future is not in the past either, this seems so simple yet many forget, they live upon the waste of their memory, they fought, they struggled, they suffered, they were victims of injustice, they are stuck in the present, they do not face it, they will die covered in mold, this I learned that day the war arrived in my village and I had to flee without looking back, so as not to waste time, now I only look forward, when I came to this camp for the displaced, there was hardly anyone here, everything around seemed to be deserted, abandoned, I said my future is here, therefore yesterday, when another government officer arrived and said that *the war had already been over for three years, we are creating the conditions for all the displaced to return to their places of origin, those who wish to return must sign up, those who do not wish return to the place from where they came can indicate any other place where they would like to be transferred, this camp is going to close down*, I looked at my wife, at my children, I thought of the cassava, the sweet potato, the lettuce and onion that I had planted, I thought about the goats and the chickens reared by my wife, about the market not far from the road, about the taxi drivers and the farms that had started to appear, about the truck drivers who had passed through here in the last few days, about my life, which, almost by itself, was emerging in this place, I looked again at the man from the government, I spoke slowly, I do not know if he understood, *I am staying right here, at least for the time being, tomorrow I can go anywhere that the future takes me, Angola is wherever I plant my field.*